# Also by Ronald Hale

## SECRETS SERIES
Secrets End (Book 1)
Secrets Begin (Book 2)
Secrets Enemy (Book 3)

Silence is the Enemy

## UPCOMING BOOKS
The Hidden Oath
Hunter's Destiny

# The Hidden Exchange

RONALD HALE

S.I.T.E.
PUBLISHING

ISBN: 979-8-9880626-5-3
LCCN: 2024922383

10 9 8 7 6 5 4 3 2 1

Printed in the United States of America
(Paperback) First Edition: March 2025


**SITE PUBLISHING**
7330 Staples Mill Road #106
Richmond, VA 23228

**Author Information**
Ronald Hale
Website: ronhalebooks.com
Email: sitepublishingtoday@gmail.com


**Cover Design:** JenC Designs
**Illustration Design:** Amanda M.

To my Lord and Savior Jesus Christ, my unfailing source of strength, peace, and purpose. May every word within these pages be a testament to Your boundless love, unending grace, and eternal truth. May this work bring glory to **You alone**.

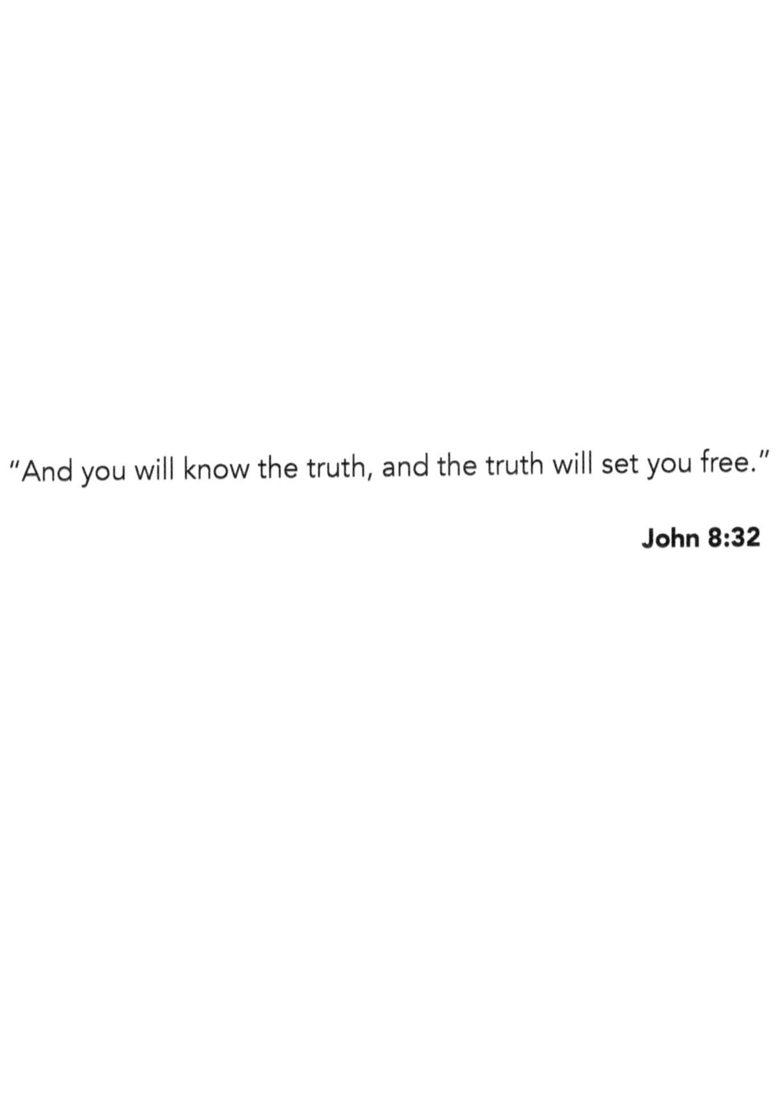

"And you will know the truth, and the truth will set you free."

**John 8:32**

# CHAPTER 1

Seeking, Searching, and Finding a Sign

I STEPPED UP TO THE CHURCH'S DOUBLE DOORS, clutching the bible against my side as if it might anchor me. My heart felt heavier than the book itself, weighed down by a growing emptiness. I took a deep breath, hoping the air might somehow soothe the ache within. Right then, I needed to hear from God more than anything else.

As I pushed the doors open, I tried to silence the doubts that were creeping in. I'd entered countless times before, looking for something real, but all I ever found were leaders twisting God's word, using fear as their tool to keep people in line. But this time had to be different, right? It just had to be!

The choir's unfamiliar melody drifted through the sanctuary, each note tugging at something deep within me. I moved down the aisle with purpose, my eyes fixed straight ahead, unwilling to meet the gaze of anyone around me. I wasn't here for them. I was here for a word from God.

Settling into my seat, about five rows from the front, I scanned the room, hoping to spot a familiar face. But as I glanced around the crowded sanctuary, I realized I was alone in this sea of strangers. I tried to focus on the service, but after two songs, the choir left the stage, and a woman stepped up, so stunning she took my breath away. Her long, flowing black hair and radiant presence lit up the room.

I shifted in my seat, my attention fixed on her. For a moment, I forgot where I was, feeling like I'd wandered into a lounge instead of the house of God. But I quickly reminded myself why I was here. This wasn't the place for wandering thoughts.

Refocusing, I turned to my left and caught the eye of an older gentleman in a sharp blue two-piece suit. His warm smile was a welcome distraction, pulling me back into the spiritual atmosphere I came for.

"This must be your first time here," the older gentleman said, sliding into the seat beside me. Leaning in, he whispered, "She's spoken for."

*Caught red-handed*, I thought, grinning awkwardly at him. My cheeks warmed as I realized I'd been caught staring. One thing was clear—I needed to get these eyes under control before I found myself being escorted out of the church for gawking at the another man's woman. But even so, there was no denying how beautiful she was.

A few minutes later, she began pacing back and forth across the stage, her eyes sweeping over the crowd as she shouted the name of Jesus with rising intensity. Her voice was powerful as it grew more intense, and then suddenly, she started speaking in a language I didn't understand. I was sure it wasn't English. It was like something had taken over her. The crowd around me leaped to their feet, cheering her on like we were at a sporting event, not in a church.

I stayed glued to my seat, unsure of what to make of it all. Then, without warning, she transitioned into singing William McDowell's classic hit, *Withholding Nothing*. The familiar melody wrapped around me, pulling me in. I closed my eyes, letting the atmosphere wash over me, and for a moment, I almost forgot where I was.

Emotion welled up inside me, and I felt tears prickling at the corners of my eyes. I quickly wiped them away, not wanting anyone to see me like that. I was lost in the moment, and the room seemed to fall into a hush, a deep, reverent silence that stretched on for what felt like hours.

When I finally opened my eyes, she was looking right at me. "You in the green and white shirt," she shouted, her voice cutting through the quiet. "Stand up."

Peering around the church like someone searching for a lost soul, she shouted again, this time with more urgency. "You, in the green and white shirt. Stand up!"

I glanced down for the first time since I'd walked into the church, and my heart skipped a beat. I was wearing a green and white shirt. Surely, she wasn't talking to me, a complete stranger. I stayed glued to my seat, trying to blend in with the crowd, my mind racing.

But she wasn't letting it go. "Yeah, that's right," she said, pointing directly at me. "I'm talking to you. Now stand up! God has a word for you."

The man beside me gave my shoulder a gentle nudge. "Get up, son," he whispered, his voice filled with encouragement.

Nodding, I reluctantly stood, wiping my sweaty palms on the side of my pants. My heart pounded in my chest like a drumbeat, each thud reminding me that all eyes were on me—and on the woman of God who had singled me out. Just an hour ago, I'd walked into this church hoping to hear a word from God, and now, here I was, caught in a moment that felt almost surreal.

As I met her gaze, the world around me seemed to fade away. She stretched her arm toward me, her voice powerful and commanding. "God said someone close to you is trying to steal your creativity. Someone close to you doesn't want you to succeed, but God is telling you this is when you are to worship Him. It's going to be hard, but I want you to know—"

Her words suddenly shifted into the unknown language she had spoken earlier, her voice rising in intensity. "God says you will not have to chase your blessings; they will chase you down. Hallelujah. God is going to protect you through this storm, my son, but He wants your worship."

With my arms raised, I felt a single tear roll down my face. "Thank you, Jesus," I whispered, my eyes still locked on the woman speaking life over me.

Then, her voice cut through the air again, more commanding this time. "Step out into the aisle and run around the pews in the church three times."

"Wait, what?" I snapped back to reality, my heart racing for a different reason now. Was she really asking me to run around the church in front of everyone? To make a fool of myself? Oh no, there was no way I was doing that.

I glanced down at my loose-fitting Levi jeans and untied Timberland boots. What if I tripped and fell? My mind raced with all the embarrassing possibilities. What if some content cre-ator caught it on video and plastered it all over TikTok, Insta-gram, or Facebook? The whole world would see me—stumbling, fumbling, making a spectacle of myself.

Heck no, I was not doing it.

But no sooner had I decided I wouldn't do it; I found myself standing in the aisle, crouched down like I was about to compete for an Olympic gold medal—except this imaginary track was all mine. If this is what God wanted from me, then so be it.

"Okay, God, I trust you," I whispered, more to myself than to anyone else. The crowd began to cheer, their voices blending into a wave of encouragement.

And then, without another thought, I took off running.

# CHAPTER 2



WITH MY UNTIED TIMBERLANDS FLOPPING ON AND off my feet, I circled the pews like a man on a mission. If this was truly God speaking to me through her, I was going to give it everything I had. As I rounded the pews a second time, feeling like a world-class sprinter, her voice rang out again, clear and firm.

"I want someone to join him!" she shouted. "God said there is power in numbers. Get up and run with him!"

At once, a short, stout man in a red warm-up suit bolted into the aisle, charging after me like a cop in hot pursuit. He was about fifty yards behind when I decided to pick up speed, determined not to let him catch me. No way was I going to let him catch me. I sprinted past him, easily lapping him like it was a real-life turtle versus hare race—only this time, the rabbit was going to win.

I was so focused on the race, I didn't even notice my pants slipping down. As I hit the final stretch of my third lap around the church, I slowed to a jog, panting hard and drenched in sweat.

Did I really just run around the church like a complete idiot in front of a crowd of strangers? But if this was truly an act of spiritual obedience, thenso be it—fool or not, I'd done what I was called to do.

Before I could take my seat, I felt a hand on my shoulder. Turning around, I saw the guy in the red warm-up suit, just as sweaty and out of breath as I was.

"My name is Sam," he said, extending his hand. "I didn't know a person could run that fast in boots without falling on their face."

We both laughed, the tension of the moment easing with the shared humor.

"Maybe it was the Holy Spirit," I found myself saying, though I wasn't entirely sure I believed it.

Just then, her voice rang out again. "Come," she called, her tone gentle yet commanding. "Come here, son."

Led to the front of the church by Sam, I quickly wiped the last bit of sweat off my brow. A group of older men dressed in all black stood before me like bodyguards, their faces stern, etched with deep wrinkles. For a brief moment, the thought crossed my mind that I could take them if it came to that, and I almost smiled. But I shook my head, chastising myself for such a thought at this crucial point in my spiritual journey.

The woman of God descended the stairs, moving toward me with a grace that made her seem even more beautiful up close. I found myself momentarily lost in her eyes, as if under some kind of spell. She began to circle me, speaking in that unknown language again, just like before. But this time, I didn't care. Maybe one day, I, too, would speak in a foreign language like hers and carry the same power and influence she seemed to wield over the crowd.

God, please don't let this be some circus show with me as the church's guinea pig, I thought, still unsure why I was standing there, feeling like the star of some spiritual reality show.

"You thought showing your face in this building tonight was an accident, didn't you?" Her voice boomed with power and conviction, and I caught a hint of cinnamon on her breath. "But God is a way maker, and tonight, your prayers will be answered." The crowd behind me erupted in cheers, their energy electrifying the room.

Out of nowhere, Sam—who had been quieter than a church mouse just moments before—broke out into a wild dance, his movements erratic, like someone in the throes of a seizure.

Without warning, he barreled past me, nearly knocking me over, and took off running around the church like a man who had just tasted freedom for the first time.

I stood there, bewildered, a flood of uncharted emotions crashing into me, threatening to send me sinking like the Titanic into an iceberg of uncertainty.

"Raise your hands in the air," she commanded, breaking into a dance of her own. Even the older men, who had been so stern and stoic moments before, began to move, hopping up and down on one leg, then the other. Two of them raised their hands in the air, and as she touched their foreheads, they dropped like dominos, one by one.

Oh, heck no! I thought, as Sam reappeared by my side, sporting a mischievous grin. "This is where the fun begins," he said, raising his hands in the air. Just like the two older men before him, he fell to the ground by her touch. I watched in horror as the three of them lay side by side on the floor. Please, God, don't let me fall for this trickery.

"Raise your hands in the air," she repeated, her voice firm. I swallowed hard, noticing a droplet of sweat clinging to her forehead. As if on cue, two men seated on the front pew rose and positioned themselves behind me.

"Don't worry, we'll catch you," one of them said, his voice calm. "Just let the Holy Spirit take over."

With a deep breath, I raised my hands in the air and closed my eyes, desperately trying to think of a way out of this spectacle. But it was too late. "Holy Spirit, take over," she chanted, slapping my hands repeatedly as if I had just scored the winning basket in an NBA championship game. But this was no game—this was real life. The slaps kept coming, over and over, until finally, she stopped.

With my hands still raised, I felt her step closer. She lifted her right hand, placed it on my forehead, and pushed. But I refused to fall like the others. My feet stayed firmly planted, and my body stiffened with resolve.

"Don't worry, we'll catch you," came the voice of one of the guys behind me. "Just fall. It'll be okay."

My body tensed up, every muscle tightening in resistance. Was I really about to play this game? To betray my conscience – and more than that, betray God? The weight of the decision bore down on me, tearing me apart inside.

As I wrestled with what was right and wrong, I felt her soft hand meet my forehead one final time. And then, the inevitable happened.

# CHAPTER 3

*For wide is the gate and broad the road*

SO THERE I WAS, SPRAWLED ON MY BACK BESIDE Sam and the other two, pretending as if the divine had just swept over me. My eyes stayed tightly shut, resisting the urge to check if anyone had seen through my act. They had to know, right? What kind of game was I playing with God? Despite this truth, I didn't move. With my arms outstretched, I calculated how long I could hold out before I'd have to get up and play the part of the dazed, touched believer. Each second dragged on, and I found myself ensnared in my own deception, the weight of guilt pressing down on me. What was I doing lying here, wrapped in a lie?

Just hand me the Oscar for this award-winning performance, I thought, stifling the urge to laugh at the absurdity of it all, but laughing was the last thing needed in this moment. I needed a deliverance, immediately.

A minute later, I cracked open my eyes and glanced to my left. Sam and the others were gone, leaving me to face the buzzing crowd alone. Two older gentlemen pulled me to my feet and practically dragged me back to my seat—a fitting end to my award-worthy charade. Embarrassment washed over me as I slumped into my seat, bowing my head in a pretense of prayer. The last thing I wanted was for someone to see through the facade and call me out for making a mockery of God. From time to time, I would open my eyes to see if someone was shaking their head at me, or, worse, if a friend or co-worker of mine witnessed my foolery. I still can't believe I ran around the church three times. Actually, that was pretty funny, even if it wasn't.

A few moments later, still lost in a cloud of doubt, I decided that enough was enough. As the woman of God continued to amaze the crowd, I grabbed my Bible, quietly slipped past the old man seated beside me, and made my way to the exit, silently begging God for forgiveness. But just as I reached the door, the guy who helped me to my feet was there, blocking my way.

"Leaving so soon?" His beady eyes tracked mine, locking me in place. "We're just getting started. The co-pastor is about to preach a powerful word of God. You can't leave before God speaks to you."

"Wait, what?" My voice trembled. "God plans to speak to me again?"

"That's why you're here, right?" He smiled, revealing a shiny gold tooth. "We're all here to hear a word from the Lord, just like Paul when he was on his road to Damascus and encountered the Lord."

"Yeah, but didn't the Lord blind him on that road?" I looked toward the exit, needing a quick way out of this place.

"You're hilarious," he slapped me on the back. "You're not really leaving, are you?"

Shrugging as a wave of melancholy washed over me, my eyes drifted past his shoulder, through the glass door, to where the other parishioners hung on the woman of God's every word. The weight of my actions pressed down on me, heavy like Judas on the night he betrayed Jesus with a kiss. What I'd just participated in felt like nothing more than a charade, a deceit meant to mislead others. How could God use me now?

"It's getting late," I said, glancing at my Apple Watch as if it might offer a reprieve.

"Forgive my rudeness, but I'm Charles Bradley, one of the elders of the church," he said, his grip firm on my arm as he steered me back to my seat. "We need brothers like you in the fold. Brothers standing on God's truth."

Was that really what he thought? That I was standing on God's truth? He couldn't have been more wrong. I wasn't standing on anything solid—I'd betrayed my own conscience and, worse, God.

The rest of the sermon dragged on like a bad dream I couldn't wake up from. I kept my head low, careful not to draw any attention. The last thing I needed was to be called out again or, God forbid, sent running around the church like last time.

She preached a message from Romans 14, stating anything that we do as believers that doesn't come from faith, is sin, and that each person should be convinced in their own mind not to do anything that goes against their conscience or the word of God.

Each word deepened the disillusionment that had taken root, and something had shifted inside me, something I couldn't ignore.

After the service, church members surrounded me, treating me like some sort of celebrity. But the memory of what had just happened clung to me like a shadow. Charles introduced me to other leaders of the church, each one urging me to join their ranks, but there was no way I would knowingly join a church that used trickery to deceive people looking for a true relationship with God. Or maybe I was wrong; maybe the leaders did have the power to make others fall with a single touch. With my back turned to the stage, I felt a hand on my shoulder. I turned to find the woman who laid holy hands on me, her eyes fixed on me with an unspoken hope.

"I'm Naomi Adams, the co-pastor of Standing on God's Truth Ministry," she said, her voice warm as she extended her perfectly manicured hand. "And you are?"

"My friends call me JB," I said, shaking her hand. "But my government name is James Barnes."

She studied me with a discerning gaze, then her face broke into a radiant smile. "God has incredible plans for your life, Brother James. The Spirit of God doesn't deceive. You're destined for great things in His name. Do you believe that?"

I turned to Charles, whose face was so intense it felt like he was trying to extract my very soul. With a hesitant nod toward Naomi, I forced the words out.

"I hope so," I said, though the doubt gnawed at me. I wasn't convinced God would want anything to do with me after tonight.

"Hope is for the birds, Brother James." Without warning, she threw her hands up and began praying in what I would later learn was tongues—one of many spiritual gifts given to believers of Jesus. It looked as if I wasn't given that gift or the ability to interpret it.

A large crowd formed around us, all with raised hands chanting in many different languages. As I stood there with my eyes closed, I was hoping she wouldn't touch me as she had before. There was no way I was falling a second time. I guess you could say I had grown a pair. Midway into her prayer, she dropped her hands on my shoulders and said words I will never forget.

"Use your servant in a way that will bring you glory. Give him the spirit of a thousand men so that he will speak to the nations. Transform him in a way he will know it's you, Jesus. Let his yes always be for your glory. As David slew Goliath with a slingshot and a stone, I pray you will fill him with your word to tear down strongholds, in the name of Jesus."

And with that, she was done praying.

"Thank you," I said softly, just enough for only her to hear.

"God told me you were going to be here tonight," she smiled lovingly, like a mother to a child. "Life as you once knew it will never be the same."

"What does that mean?" I was confused.

"Just be still, my son, and know that God is God. May the peace of God be with you always."

After meeting the other church leaders, Charles and Sam walked me out to the parking lot.

"I hope to see you on Sunday," Sam said, giving me a playful jab in the chest.

"Maybe," I muttered, pressing the unlock button on my truck key, and contemplating what the co-pastor meant about my life never being the same again. What was the mystery behind her words?

As I sat in the driver's seat, replaying the night's events, I overheard Sam say to Charles, "I believe he's the one."

Pulling out of the parking lot, I lit up a Black and Mild cigar and rolled down the windows as the smoke drifted out. There was something different about this church, something that lingered in the back of my mind, refusing to be brushed aside. Despite how it started, I knew I needed to know more. Maybe God was trying to get my attention, but for my life, I didn't understand why God would give everyone in the church the gift of speaking in tongues except me.

# CHAPTER 4



"WHAT DO YOU MEAN YOU RAN AROUND THE CHURCH three times?" Will was laughing so hard I could hear him choking through the phone. "And then you laid out on the church floor like you'd just been zapped by the Holy Ghost?"

I knew telling him was a mistake. "It's not funny, man," I grumbled, even though I could feel a smirk tugging at my lips.

"You're kidding, right?" he wheezed. "You were out there doing laps like it was track practice, and then you went full method actor on the floor? Man, I'd have paid to see that!"

Will was my best friend, the only person I trusted more than myself. I figured he'd get it, maybe even sympathize a little with the pressure I was under—or at least not laugh in my face. Everyone has weak moments, right? But judging by the way he was laughing like a maniac through the phone, it was clear I wasn't getting any sympathy tonight. This story was going to be his go-to joke for years.

"Please tell me you're joking," Will said, laughing even louder.

Before I could respond, the FaceTime prompt lit up on my phone. I hesitated but accepted the call.

"This is no laughing matter," I said, trying to sound serious as I turned into the parking lot of Kroger's grocery store, nearly side-swiping an older woman with a cart full of groceries. After settling into a parking spot, I pulled my phone from the car holder and headed inside, with Will still cracking up on the other end.

"I know you're not wearing slacks with that shirt," he said, his voice full of disbelief. "Tell me you at least had on sneakers."

"Nope," I sighed, bracing myself for his reaction. "I was wearing Timbs."

Will lost it. "Please tell me you didn't humiliate yourself in front of the entire church by running around in Timbs. Tell me it isn't so."

"It is," I groaned, feeling the embarrassment wash over me again. "Full-on laps, in Timbs. The whole church probably thought I was auditioning for a construction site musical."

I had had enough. "Listen," I said, grabbing a cart as I entered the store. "I'm confiding in you as my boy. This is no laughing matter. I think I sinned against God, and now I'm fearing for my soul."

"Stop," Will managed to say between bouts of laughter, tears streaming down his face. "We need to take this show on the road. You're funnier than Kevin Hart. First, you run around the church thinking you had a spiritual encounter, and then you and three other grown men are passed out on the floor after the pastor blows on the three of you. Is that what you're telling me?"

"Unfortunately, yeah," I mumbled, trying to keep a straight face as I tossed a loaf of bread into my cart.

"Man," Will wheezed, "if that's what getting right with God looks like, I'm staying a sinner. I've seen some wild stuff, but you…you're on another level, JB."

"I'm serious, Will. What if I really messed up?" I pushed the cart down the aisle, trying to avoid eye contact with other shoppers who might have heard my loud friend's commentary.

"Look," Will said, finally catching his breath. "If God didn't strike you down mid-lap, I think you're gonna be okay. But seriously, next time, leave the Timbs at home."

"She didn't blow on us," I snapped, rolling my eyes even though he couldn't see me. "She nudged the three of us on the forehead, and like dominos, we fell one by one."

Will was still laughing. Why was he still laughing?

"And while you were laying there, what were you thinking?"

Out of nowhere, I started laughing too. It was pretty comical, now that I thought about it.

"I was thinking about how long I should stay down before getting up, pretending to be all dazed like I'd just taken a hit from Floyd Mayweather."

There was a long pause, and then he finally spoke. "Hold on a minute, JB," he chuckled, and the screen went black.

A moment later, he was back, but this time, he wasn't alone. His wife had joined him, both of them grinning from ear to ear.

"Tell my wife what you just told me," he said, barely holding back his laughter. "And don't leave out a single detail."

"Oh, I get it," I said, stopping in front of the produce aisle. "You two are teaming up to clown me, huh?"

"JB," she chimed in, "were you really laying on the floor in the position of Jesus on the Cross? Please tell me you have more respect for God than that."

Shaking my head, I couldn't help but smile, even though I was cringing inside. "I hope you both have a good night." And with that, I ended the call, praying God still had plans for my life after the stunt I pulled at church.

# CHAPTER 5



THE NEXT DAY, I WAS UP BRIGHT AND EARLY, TRYING to psych myself up for the day. But honestly, who was I fooling? I still couldn't get over the fact that I'd run around that church like Usain Bolt in front of a bunch of strangers. What on earth was I thinking? Trying to prove something? If so, I'm not sure what it was, because there was nothing spiritual about my antics. It was outright crazy. But hey, I guess you could call me a fool for Christ, or at least that's what I was telling myself, even though I didn't believe it.

Lying across the bed, with my arms behind my head, I stared up at the ceiling fan, hoping that somehow, it would inspire me to get up and start my day. Spoiler alert: all it did was lull me back to sleep like a baby in a crib. It wasn't until my alarm clock buzzed me out of dreamland that I finally shot out of bed, feeling more like a zombie from a horror movie than a man ready to seize the day. I groggily stumbled into the master bathroom for my morning routine.

It was 6:30 a.m., and the day was already off to a rough start.

At 8:00 a.m., I grabbed my keys from the bowl in the hall, took a deep breath, and stepped outside, determined to face whatever the world had in store for me. After last night's spectacle, some redemption was definitely needed. My first stop before work, Dunkin Donuts—a place that quickly became my drug of choice from the moment I stepped foot on corporate grounds. Somehow, I convinced myself that a daily cup of coffee was the antidote to survive the workday.

The drive-thru line was longer than usual, so I pulled into an empty spot near the entrance and decided to go inside. And that's when I saw her—co-pastor Naomi, looking just as radiant as the night before. What on earth was she doing on my side of town? And more importantly, where was her husband?

My heart raced, and without a second thought, I spun on my heels, planning a swift exit before she noticed me. But, of course, fate had other plans. I collided straight into Sam, who had a grin on his face as if he'd just caught me doing something I wasn't supposed to.

This couldn't be good.

"Brother James!" Sam's voice boomed through Dunkin Donuts like a crazed fan at a football game. Heads turned, and I felt the heat of all eyes zeroing in on me like I was a dartboard—and when Naomi spotted me, bullseye. Were they here together?

"What's up?" I said, trying not to let my awkwardness show.

"What are you doing on this side of town?" He slapped me on the back with enough force to knock the wind out of me, but his grin said he was only half-serious. "And look who's here—co-pastor too. What are the odds?"

"Oh, so you guys aren't… together?" I asked, maybe a bit too eager.

He shook his head with a quick smile. "Nah, she was here first. I'm running late, though. I'll catch up with you Sunday." He stepped to the front of the line, gave Naomi a quick hug, then turned to me. As he headed for the door, he flashed a peace sign. "Later, man," he called out, and then bolted out the door like he was on a mission.

Jumping out of line, Naomi floated toward me, all smiles. "Look what the cat dragged in," she almost purred, her eyes twinkling. "Fancy seeing you here, man of God."

I glanced over my shoulder, half-hoping she was talking to someone else. *Man of God?* Was she referring to me? Maybe she meant "track star." And please, for the love of everything holy, don't tell me you've heard from God again, and this time, He wants me to sprint around Dunkin Donuts' parking lot. The thought nearly made me laugh out loud.

Instead, I just nodded and smiled, trying to hide the fact that I was low-key praying for an escape plan.

"Leaving so soon?" Her eyes locked onto mine, a knowing glint in them. "You just got here."

"Uh, I think I left my wallet in the car," I stammered, glancing toward the exit like it held the promise of freedom. I knew better, though. My wallet was right there in my hand—bonehead move.

Her smile widened, and she tilted her head. "So... what's that in your hand?"

I froze, caught like a deer in headlights. *Of course, she noticed,* I thought, mentally kicking myself. "Oh, this?" I laughed nervously, waving the wallet like it had magically appeared. "Just... keeping it close. You never know these days."

"Mmmmhmmm," she shook her head with a knowing laugh. "You do remember I'm a pastor, right? Lying to a woman of the cloth is never a good thing, Brother James. But like God, I forgive you… this time."

I chuckled, scratching the back of my neck. "I appreciate the grace. I'm still a work in progress."

She gave me that *I know* look, then stepped closer. "Well, don't run off too quickly. There's a reason you're here today. God always has a plan."

I glanced back at the door, wishing for a divine escape route, but something told me I wasn't going to get off that easy.

"I guess I can spare a few minutes," I said, stepping in line next to her.

"Good morning, James," the barista called out with a bright smile, leaning over the counter. "Medium coffee, cream with two sugars, right?"

"Yup," I grinned back. "And add two coconut donuts with that."

She raised an eyebrow and smirked. "Looks like someone's not watching his figure today. Anything else?"

I laughed and motioned toward Naomi, who was studying the menu like it held the secrets of the universe. "My friend Naomi would like to order too. It's on me."

Naomi blinked in surprise, finally tearing her eyes from the menu. "You don't have to do that, Brother James," she said, but there was a glimmer of gratitude in her tone.

"Nah, I insist. Consider it... redemption."

"Big spender," Naomi teased, giving my back a light slap before turning to the barista. "Well, since you're so generous, I'll have a medium French vanilla iced coffee and a blueberry muffin, butter on the side."

The barista rang us up and glanced at me. "That'll be $17.23."

Just as I reached for my wallet, Naomi's hand shot out, slipping a crisp twenty onto the counter. "Keep the change," she said with a grin.

I blinked, caught off guard. "Wait, I thought I was treating…"

Naomi just smirked, handing me my coffee and donuts like she had planned this all along. "My pleasure," she said smoothly, as if it was no big deal.

I accepted the items, trying to hide my surprise, while she grabbed her muffin and iced coffee. Then, without missing a beat, she slipped her arm through mine and steered us toward a quiet booth in the back. The smell of coffee and baked goods filled the air, but I couldn't ignore the sinking realization—I was definitely going to be late for work.

Naomi's beauty hit me like a punch to the gut. For half a second, I forgot she was a married woman. It was the first time I found myself staring at someone I knew I shouldn't want. Forbidden fruit, right there in front of me.

"So, Brother James," she said, leaning in with a smile that could melt ice. "Tell me your story."

I wasn't expecting that. My brain short-circuited for a second. What did she want to know about my story? What was she up to? And why were my palms suddenly slick with sweat? Where was her husband?

I cleared my throat, fumbling with the lid of my coffee, hoping to find some composure at the bottom of that cup. "There's not much to tell," I muttered, trying to downplay it.

I brought the cup to my lips, desperate for the familiar comfort of caffeine, but before I could take a sip, her hand gently pressed down on mine, stopping me mid-sip.

"Are you going to pray for our food?" she asked, eyebrows raised as if I'd just committed a serious offense.

I froze, coffee still in hand, as she gave me a look that said she wasn't going to let this slide.

Before I could respond, she slipped her hands into mine, closed her eyes, and bowed her head. I swallowed hard, feeling the weight of the moment settle in.

Sighing, I mumbled, "God, thank you for this food we are about to receive, and for Naomi's kindness in purchasing it, even though I was supposed to treat her... but, you know, I'm thankful." At that, she let out a soft chuckle, and I couldn't help but grin.

"I'm thankful for our connection, and, uh… I pray you forgive me for sinning against you. I'm sorry. Amen."

When I opened my eyes, I went straight for the donut like it was the answer to all my problems, biting in as if that powdered sugar held some kind of divine solution.

"Thank you for that wonderful prayer," Naomi said, her hand lingering on mine, gently rubbing it in slow circles. The warmth was both comforting and nerve-wracking. "Before you share your story, I need to tell you something."

Her grip tightened, and I watched as her expression shifted. Her eyes grew heavy with emotion, and a single tear slipped down her cheek.

"What's wrong?"

"My husband and I…," she said, stopping mid-sentence, and suddenly, the tears were falling freely.

I froze, completely caught off guard. My mind scrambled for the right response, but I just stared at her, feeling like a man trapped in quicksand with no way out. Then, in a move that surprised even me, I stood up. Without thinking, I reached out and caught her tears before they hit the table, pulling her into an embrace. It was instinct, or maybe it was something else. Either way, it felt right in that moment—comforting her, or maybe comforting myself.

Her eyes met mine, and for a split second, time slowed. She traced a finger along my cheek, her touch soft and deliberate. My heart raced as I licked my lips, feeling the weight of what was about to happen.

Just as her lips parted and we leaned in, my phone blared in my pocket, shattering the moment like glass. I jumped back, fumbling for it as if my life depended on answering. Naomi blinked, wiping the last of her tears, while I glanced down at the screen. It was Will.

Of all times.

"Uh, I—I have to take this," I stammered, stepping back. The tension in the air could've been cut with a knife, but I wasn't ready to face whatever this was.

Naomi nodded, her expression unreadable, as I turned away and pressed the answer button. Will's laughter exploded through the phone.

"Bro, did I catch you at a bad time? Don't tell me you're sprinting around your office like you did at church last night?"

I closed my eyes, letting out a slow breath. "Not. Now."

# CHAPTER 6

*God will give you a way out of temptation*

"YOU'RE PLAYING WITH FIRE, MAN." WILL'S VOICE CUT through the noise of the coffee shop, his tone dead serious. "Listen, stay away from her, and don't set foot in that church again. First, she's got you running laps like you're possessed, and now, if I hadn't called, you'd be crossing the line with the pastor's wife. Bro, you're too smart to be this dumb. What's really going on with you?"

I felt the weight of his words settle in. My mind flashed back to Naomi's tear-filled eyes, her hand resting on mine, the way she leaned in close. My throat tightened. Will wasn't wrong, and no matter how I tried to spin it, there was no justifying what almost happened. I leaned back in my seat, running a hand over my face, trying to shake the guilt creeping in.

This wasn't from the Lord—this had temptation written all over it. And here I was, sitting in Dunkin Donuts, on the verge of sinning with a married woman. I glanced around the shop, the smell of fresh coffee and donuts doing little to calm my nerves. My heart pounded in my chest. At this rate, I could practically feel the heat from the lake of fire.

"Everything happened so fast," I stumbled over the words, my heartbeat still racing. "One minute she's asking about my life, the next... I'm holding her, and—" I stopped, feeling the heat creep into my face. "Man, you were right." I shook my head, half-smiling. "I was about to kiss her. I barely dodged it, thanks to your call."

Will's sigh echoed through the phone. "You know the story of Adam and Eve, right?"

My eyes darted to the ceiling as I tried to shake off the tension. "Yeah, man. Who doesn't?" But even as I spoke, the ghost of Naomi's touch lingered on my skin. I could still picture her tear-streaked face, and the way her lips had almost met mine. "Get behind me, Satan," I muttered, but the words felt hollow, like I was trying to convince myself more than anything.

"And you remember how that ended for them?" Will pressed, his voice pulling me back to reality.

"Yeah, they were kicked out of the Garden of Eden, and from the presence of God, too, right?" I uttered, rubbing my hand over my face, as if that could wipe away the lingering guilt.

"Yup," Will's voice deepened. "And if you're not careful, Heaven's door might not be open for you either."

His sudden change in tone made me pause, but then his laughter broke through the line. "She must be hella good-looking, though. Send me a picture of her."

I blinked, caught off guard. "What?" My grip tightened around the phone as my brain scrambled to switch gears. "We're talking about Heaven shutting its door on me, and now you want a picture of my... sin mate?" My voice faded in disbelief. I leaned back against the chair, shaking my head at the absurdity of it all. "You're tripping, Will. Later."

"Peace, JB," he said, his laughter still echoing in my ear. "And remember what I said. Stay away from her and that church."

Just as I was about to hang up, his voice came through once more, teasing. "Oh, and don't forget to send me a picture of her."

After the call ended, I turned back to Naomi. Her eyes, glistening with unshed tears, seemed to plead with me to stay. I could feel the weight of the moment pressing down on me, and despite the undeniable pull I felt toward her, I knew I had to walk away.

"I'm sorry," I said, the words barely leaving my lips. They felt hollow, empty, like an attempt to patch up something that was already broken. My heart pounded, caught between regret and a desire I couldn't ignore. This wasn't just a mistake—it felt like a test, one I was failing miserably. Will's warning echoed in my mind, sharp and clear, and suddenly the weight of the moment was too much. It felt like everything around me was caving in, dragging me deeper into a mess I wasn't sure I could escape.

Naomi's silence hung in the air, her gaze fixed on the floor, avoiding mine. She didn't need to say a word; the quiet between us was louder than any argument, heavier than any apology. It said everything neither of us was brave enough to admit.

Taking a steadying breath, I glanced at Naomi one last time. "Goodbye," I said, my voice low but firm. I didn't wait for a response—I couldn't. Without looking back, I turned and walked out of Dunkin' Donuts.

# CHAPTER 7



FOR THE NEXT SEVERAL MONTHS, I MADE IT A POINT to steer clear of Pastor Naomi and her church. I'd be lying if I said I didn't miss her—more than anyone or anything I'd ever known. But deep down, I knew that being entangled with a married woman wasn't part of God's plan for me. It was a trap, one carefully laid by the enemy.

In those months of absence, I visited other churches, searching for God and, in a way, searching for myself. I wasn't lost, not exactly, but there was something missing. And while I couldn't put my finger on it, I knew one thing for sure—I needed God, perhaps more than ever.

Most of the leaders in the churches I visited were more interested in prosperity than salvation. Their sermons were filled with promises of wealth, healing, and success, as long as you left a generous offering. The more money you gave, the more blessings they claimed God would pour out on you. It felt less like worship and more like a transaction, as if God's favor could be bought and sold.

I sat through sermon after sermon, listening to pastors peddling their personal agendas, pushing people toward worldly riches instead of the resurrection power of Jesus. Their messages were wrapped in glossy packaging, but they were hollow on the inside. It reminded me of what the Apostle Paul warned against when he said, "We do not peddle the word of God for profit." Yet, here they were, offering houses, cars, and job promotions as if God were a vending machine and faith was the currency.

I couldn't shake the feeling that it was all wrong.

And it worked. People lined up, desperate, clutching envelopes filled with hundreds, sometimes thousands of dollars, tears streaming down their faces as they cried out in the name of Jesus. The leaders stood at the front, each claiming to hold a divine title—Apostle, Prophet, Pastor, or Evangelist—promising that God's healing power flowed through them. They spoke with authority, hands raised high, telling the crowd that their miracles were just one "faith seed" away.

But for those who couldn't or wouldn't give, the message was clear: their faith wasn't strong enough. The leaders would point fingers, telling them they'd stay in their broken state until their offering was acceptable in the eyes of God. It was spiritual manipulation at its finest, and the people believed it.

What had become of the people, and the church of God? These leaders, preaching riches instead of the glory of God through Jesus, were growing wealthier while the congregation grew poorer—clinging to promises that would never come. And what about me?

Doubt crept in as I watched the charade. Was my desire to serve God just an illusion? Would I, too, end up like the others—waiting for a leader to speak, hoping their words were from God Himself? The thought of one day standing in that same line, trading money for a blessing, gnawed at me. Would I be like them, placing my faith in empty promises, all for the sake of chasing prosperity?

As I watched the money pile up on the altar, doubt hit me like a wave. Everything I had ever been taught about God felt distant, almost foreign. In that moment, something shifted. Watching the scene unfold before me, I knew—I needed to repent. If I was ever going to truly find God, I had to have my own Damascus

Road experience. Something real. Something that would shake me to my core and bring me back to the truth.

During the altar call service, as people made their way to the front to dedicate their lives to God, I stayed seated on the balcony. With my head bowed, I silently prayed. "God, deliver me from being a people pleaser," I whispered. "Use me to bring glory to Your name." In that still moment, I sought clarity, hoping for a breakthrough, asking God to guide my steps and give me purpose beyond the surface.

# CHAPTER 8

*A message in the form of a vision*

THE COMPANY'S ANNUAL SALES CONFERENCE WAS just three days away in New York, and I'd been invited as one of the guest speakers, with all expenses covered. However, flying wasn't my thing—my fear of heights, or rather falling, made it hard to enjoy. So, I chose to drive the five-hour trek in my new F-150, a truck I had treated myself to a few months back. It was part of a pact I made with myself—to buy something expensive each year, something no one else would get for me. Last year, it was a Suzuki Boulevard motorcycle.

I'd packed the night before, and the excitement of a few days in New York had me buzzing. New York was my kind of city—vibrant, energetic, and full of life. God knew I needed a change of scenery, and this trip was just what I'd been craving.

At 7 a.m., I stumbled into the master bathroom, still half-asleep, as *Empire State of Mind* blared from my Bose speaker. I sang along, hitting the high notes as best as I could—though Jay-Z and Alicia Keys probably didn't need my help.

I caught my reflection in the mirror. Bedhead, puffy eyes. But for a second, I was somewhere else—sipping red wine, or maybe a cold beer, while a T-bone steak and roasted veggies sat in front of me.

The thought of it all—good food, great company, and the thrill of a Knicks game—had me practically vibrating with anticipation. The city was calling, and I couldn't wait to answer.

As the warm water rinsed away the suds of my shower gel, a voice cut through the sound of the running water.

"You are tired and should lie down."

I froze. Had I really heard that, or was the steam playing tricks on me? I shook my head, brushing it off as my imagination, and turned back to the shower. The warm water streamed down, and I tried to lose myself in its steady rhythm. *Empire State of Mind* faded into the background, replaced by the soft, soulful strains of *Jireh*. The worship song wrapped around me like a comforting hug, grounding me, pulling me back to normal—or at least close to it.

But then, the voice returned, more insistent this time: "You are tired and should lay down."

I paused, feeling a chill despite the warmth of the shower. I had deliberately gone to bed early the night before, anticipating the long drive ahead. I was rested, or at least I thought I was. The voice seemed out of place, a stark contrast to my upbeat mood and the excitement I felt about the trip.

Shaking off the unsettling feeling, I let myself get caught up in the lyrics of *Jireh*, focusing on the excitement of the adventure ahead. Yet, the voice lingered in the back of my mind, an echo that seemed to push against my plans for the day.

It was supposed to be a great day, and I was pumped about hitting the road. But as soon as I stepped out of the shower, I was hit by a wave of sleepiness, like I'd been knocked out by Mike Tyson. All the energy I had just moments ago seemed to drain away instantly.

Instead of drying off, I wrapped a towel around my waist and dragged myself to the bedroom. My legs felt like lead with each step. As soon as I reached the bed, I collapsed face-first into the sheets. The world outside dissolved into nothing, and before I could think about my plans for the day, sleep overtook me completely.

When I opened my eyes, sweat clung to my skin, and my hands trembled uncontrollably. The clock on the bedside table read 10:52 p.m. I couldn't believe it—I'd been out for over fifteen hours. The dream still gripped me, its intensity leaving me shaken to the core.

I jumped out of bed, my heart hammering in my chest. In a daze, I stumbled into the kitchen, hoping for some kind of explanation. The clocks on the microwave and stove stared back at me, their identical glowing numbers confirming it: 10:52 p.m.

I rubbed my eyes, willing it to make sense, but the clocks didn't budge. They just sat there, unbothered, like the whole situation wasn't completely insane.

Back in my bedroom, still trembling, I sank to the edge of the bed. I closed my eyes and prayed, my voice shaky as I asked, "What am I supposed to do with what you showed me?"

The response was clear and simple: "Write it all down."

The New York trip would have to wait. I pulled on a t-shirt and gym shorts, feeling the weight of the unexpected shift in plans. I grabbed my laptop from the corner of my bedroom, where it lay buried in my bookbag. Sitting at my desk, I began typing furiously, pouring out every detail of the dream as vividly as I remembered it.

Hours slipped by as I powered through three cups of coffee, each one sharpening my focus. The only sound in the room was the clacking of my keyboard.

The sun dipped lower, and my fingers finally stopped. I stared at the screen, the words I'd typed now staring back at me, heavy and unmoving.

"Now what?" The words slipped out before I could stop them, but they felt as empty as the silence that filled the room.

I waited. Nothing. The stillness stretched, thick and unyielding. I scrolled through the document again, my hands shaking as each word seemed to weigh more than the last. The fear in my chest tightened, slow and insistent.

I whispered the words again, but they dissolved into the quiet. Only the soft hum of the laptop and the distant chirping of birds outside broke the silence, while the world continued on, oblivious to my stillness. the sun set, I finished typing and stared at the screen, my words filling the document.

The room felt smaller as I read and reread the dream's details. Every word, every image, pressed against me, too vivid, too clear to be just a random thought. It couldn't have been a dream. Could it?

I scrolled through the document again, searching for something, anything that would make sense of it.

Then it hit me. The message was unmistakable: I had to follow through. A chill crept up my spine, my hands frozen above the keyboard. I hesitated, then typed the title: *Struggle.*

# CHAPTER 9



I ZOOMED DOWN THE NEW JERSEY TURNPIKE, THE tires on the road creating a steady rhythm that matched my growing excitement. With less than ninety minutes to go before hitting the city, I felt a surge of energy run through me, like a kid on a sugar high. The long sleep from the day before had worked wonders. I was wide awake, feeling unstoppable—like I could take on the world.

The only thing missing was the company. The empty passenger seat next to me felt like a reminder of what I didn't have. I imagined glancing over and seeing someone smiling back at me, sharing this adventure. Maybe someday. I whispered a quick prayer, half hopeful, half doubtful, for God to send someone—someone to share this life with. Marriage seemed like a long shot, but wasn't that what faith was about? Believing in what seemed impossible?

My mind drifted to Naomi, as it had a hundred times since our encounter. No matter how much I tried to shake her, she clung to my thoughts. It wasn't just her beauty—though she was stunning, with her captivating eyes and a smile that could light up a room—it was something more. Was I wrong to hope she might be the one? I knew so little about her, but that didn't stop me from wondering and imagining. What was it about her that I couldn't let go?

The road stretched ahead, and even as I pushed forward, part of me felt stuck, tangled in thoughts of Naomi. Was it God's plan, or was I just fooling myself?

Five miles from the George Washington Bridge, I felt a strange sense of relief wash over me. I was so close to New York, and soon, all my worries would be behind me—or so I thought as I glanced at the skyline. The spot where the Twin Towers once stood caught my eye. My chest tightened, and a wave of sadness hit me like a punch to the gut. 9/11 was a day that would never fade, the kind that left a scar on the soul. I stared at the empty space in the sky, my mind heavy with memories of that fateful day and the cruelty of it all. The longer I stared, the more the sadness morphed into anger, boiling just beneath the surface. How could something so senseless, so devastating, have happened? My hands gripped the steering wheel tighter as the anger simmered inside me. But I couldn't let it take over. Not now. Not while I was still on this road, heading toward something that was supposed to lift me out of this darkness.

For the next twenty minutes, my mind wandered, trapped in the lives of those who had been in the towers that morning. What were they doing? Laughing over coffee, stuck in meetings, calling loved ones? And what about those on the planes? What went through their minds in those final moments? Did they know it was the end? Would they have done anything differently if they had known?

Before I could shake myself free from those heavy thoughts, I was already pulling up to the Four Seasons. Grateful for the all-expenses-paid trip, I went for the VIP treatment, starting with valet parking. If I was going to be here, I might as well enjoy it.

"Welcome to the Four Seasons, Mr. Barnes," the valet said with a smile that seemed just a bit too familiar, handing me a sleek Gold VIP card. "The attendants will take care of your luggage and bring it to your room." He opened my door with a smooth, practiced motion. "Enjoy your stay."

As I stepped out of the truck, something didn't sit right. How did he know my name? I hadn't said a word yet. Scratching my head, I barely had time to process before two well-dressed attendants opened the grand double doors with perfect synchronization.

"Welcome to the Four Seasons," they chimed in unison, their polished smiles almost robotic.

"Thanks," I replied, still feeling like something was off.

Walking into the Four Seasons felt like entering another world—one dripping with luxury. The cool marble floors gleamed under the soft lighting, leading up to towering ceilings that made everything feel grand. Sleek furnishings and modern art were perfectly placed, while massive flower arrangements filled the air with a light, sweet fragrance. I could almost smell the money.

But my room? That was the real prize. Floor-to-ceiling windows stretched across the walls, revealing a stunning view of the city that seemed endless. Plush seating, a king-size bed draped in crisp white linens, and the embrace of complete silence wrapped me in total comfort. Now, this was the life.

After a long, hot shower that washed away the miles of the drive, I settled into the room and ordered room service. A medium-well ribeye, mashed potatoes, asparagus, and a glass of chardonnay—it was the perfect way to wrap up the day.

As I sat back, the smell of the steak filling the room, I heard something outside my door that made me pause—a voice, familiar and unmistakable.

It couldn't be.

# CHAPTER 10

## Be strong and courageous

I MUST BE HEARING THINGS, I THOUGHT, SHAKING IT off as I closed the door and took another sip of wine to steady my nerves. Trying to distract myself, I grabbed the remote from the bedside table and flipped through the channels, landing on SportsCenter. The low murmur of the TV, paired with the wine, began to lull me to sleep. It had been a long day, and the highlights blurred into the background as sleep took over.

Morning light spilled through the floor-to-ceiling windows, bathing the room in a soft glow. I paced back and forth, notes in hand, while the muffled city sounds outside—traffic, faint horns—blurred into the background. Inside, the quiet tension tightened in my chest. I glanced at the clock. Still early, but time felt like it was slipping away.

My fingers gripped the edges of the note cards, the corners starting to bend under the pressure. I'd given this talk a hundred times before, **"What Are You Waiting For?"**—a speech meant to ignite passion, to push people to take that leap of faith. Normally, it was second nature to me. But today, my mind was restless. Maybe it was the idea of staring down rows of suits, socialites with sharp eyes, and corporate executives sizing me up. It was different from my usual crowd.

I inhaled deeply, trying to steady my heartbeat, and reminded myself: **"Speak to inspire, not to impress."** The words felt hollow this time, though, as if my confidence had slipped out the door with room service.

Dressed in my favorite custom blue suit, the fabric stretched comfortably over my muscular frame, enhancing the sharp lines of my physique. The classic white shirt underneath had my initials embroidered on the cuff, adding a touch of personalized elegance. My matching blue and white Retro Air Jordans peeked out from beneath the hem of my trousers, a nod to my roots and a personal flair. Growing up, dress shoes were a luxury we couldn't afford, so sneakers became my only choice. Now, wearing them with my suits isn't just style—it's a reminder of my past and a declaration of who I am today.

A fresh haircut and a carefully trimmed beard, now just a hint of a five o'clock shadow, completed my look. As I surveyed my reflection, the excitement to make a difference today began to overshadow my earlier nerves. I was ready to step onto that stage and inspire someone, at least one person, with the message I had prepared.

After popping a few Altoids, I took a moment to pray. I needed God's guidance for today, just like every other time I'd faced a challenge.

Minutes later, I found myself mingling in the lobby with an array of wealthy men and women who seemed to have no clue who I was. I flashed a confident smile and struck up conversations with anyone who met my gaze. To them, I was just another face in the crowd, possibly an affirmative action case.

I scanned the room for a familiar face from my organization but found none. Puzzled, I checked my phone again to see if the agenda had been sent. Just then, I felt a light tap on my shoulder. Turning around, I was stunned to see Naomi standing there.

"What are you doing here?" I asked, my surprise evident.

# CHAPTER 11

*Gin makes me do what I don't want to do*

"IT'S GOOD TO SEE YOU TOO," NAOMI SAID, SHAKING her head with a playful smile as she lightly tapped my arm. I stood frozen, my mind spinning, trying to make sense of the odds. What were the chances of us being in the same place, at the same time, miles away from home? A bead of sweat ran down my back. *Get it together, James,* I scolded myself, but it was too late. Panic had already crept onto my face, and she must've seen it.

There she was, standing just inches away, her radiant smile as disarming as ever. Her presence stirred something in me, something that had been simmering beneath the surface. I had prayed for her only hours ago—had God actually answered?

Before I could process any of it, Naomi stepped forward, her arms slipping around my neck as if this was the most natural thing in the world. She hugged me tightly, like we were long-lost friends—no, more like lovers reunited after years apart. My heart raced in my chest as I awkwardly returned the embrace, trying to keep my thoughts from spiraling.

Everything seemed to slow down as we stood there, wrapped in each other's arms like newlyweds in the middle of the crowded lobby. My heart pounded, but I couldn't deny the truth—it was great to see her. She looked even more stunning than the last time we crossed paths at Dunkin' Donuts. Right then, it was as if the rest of the world had faded away, leaving just the two of us. Her skin was soft, and she smelled of fresh, exotic fruit, a scent that pulled me in even closer. I held onto her like she was something irreplaceable, something I couldn't bear to lose.

Before we ended up in the New York Times gossip section, I quickly let go and took a step back, glancing around to make sure her husband wasn't lurking nearby. He had to be here somewhere, right? My hands were suddenly clammy, and I discreetly wiped them on the sides of my pants. I couldn't help but stare at her, momentarily lost in her stunning appearance like she was the star of some reality show. She wore a fitted blue dress that stopped just above her knees, paired with a pearl necklace that added a touch of class. Her high heels accentuated her toned calves, and her long ponytail, perfectly sleek, cascaded down the middle of her back. Her makeup? Absolutely flawless. She was the kind of woman who turned heads the moment she walked into a room, and from the looks of it, she was fully aware of the attention she was getting.

She stood just a few feet away, chatting casually with an older black couple, but her eyes were locked on me, like I was her favorite meal. My heart raced. There was no way this was destiny, right? No way I was supposed to be connected to a married woman, even though my messed-up mind wanted to believe it. I had to snap out of it. Smiling awkwardly, I said, "I'll be right back." Before she could reply, I spun on my heels and made a beeline for the men's bathroom, weaving through the crowd like a celebrity trying to escape the paparazzi.

In the bathroom, I leaned over the sink and let the cool water rush over my hands before splashing it on my face. The chill jolted me, but my mind kept racing. "What is she doing here?" I muttered to myself, staring at my reflection. The chances of Naomi showing up at the same event felt too wild to be a coincidence.

Of all the places she could've been, it had to be here, today, just when I needed my focus the most. My palms were sweaty again, and the familiar nervousness crept up. I couldn't back out now. I took a deep breath, closed my eyes, and whispered a prayer.

"God, I don't get it. Is this what you're doing? Did you set this up for a reason?"

As I stood there, my mind whirling with thoughts about Naomi, the door to one of the stalls creaked open. Out stepped a heavy-set guy, adjusting his belt, a goofy smirk on his face like he'd overheard everything.

"You good, buddy?" he asked, pressing the gel button at the sink. "Must be one heck of a looker—you've got that 'deer in headlights' thing going on."

I ignored him, though he wasn't wrong. Drying my hands, I tried to shake the awkwardness, but before I could collect myself, the bathroom door swung open again. Two sharply dressed men strolled in, and one of them locked eyes with me, sizing me up like I was about to do something sketchy. His gaze sent a wave of unease down my spine, making the bathroom suddenly feel way too small.

Figuring I was reading too much into it, I shrugged off the tension and headed toward the exit, ready to rejoin the event. But just as my hand reached for the door, I felt a firm tug on my arm.

It was the guy who had been glaring at me.

I spun around, teeth clenched, ready for a confrontation. "What?" I snapped, feeling my fists tighten.

He gave me a once-over. "Where do I know you from?" His eyes narrowed as if trying to place me.

"You must have me confused with someone else," I said, gripping the door handle, clearly irritated.

Before I could leave, the other guy chimed in, his face lighting up. "You're that running back for the New York Giants, right?" His voice was filled with excitement, completely misreading the situation.

As the two men continued to throw out every name they could think of, trying to pin down who I was, I decided enough was enough. "Look, I'm not who you think I am. I'm just a regular guy with a job. As much as I'd like to keep this conversation going, I've got other important things to handle. Enjoy your day, gentlemen." I gave a light chuckle as I exited the bathroom, feeling a strange sense of satisfaction. It wasn't the worst thing in the world to be mistaken for a pro athlete.

When I walked back into the lobby, Naomi was deep in conversation with a striking blonde and a distinguished gray-haired man in a black tuxedo. This was my chance to make a discreet exit before Naomi noticed me. I grabbed a bottle of water and a bagel from the open bar, then made my way towards the conference room, where the event was set to unfold. Just as I reached the door, a pair of warm hands covered my eyes, accompanied by a familiar, soothing scent.

"Guess who?" came the playful voice.

# CHAPTER 12

*the truth will set you free*

"NOW THAT I HAVE YOU ALL TO MYSELF," NAOMI SAID, lowering herself into the chair across from me. She leaned forward, her eyes narrowing playfully as she rested her chin on her hand. "I was beginning to think I'd need to send out a search party. Haven't seen you at church in months. Where've you been hiding?"

I hesitated, then let a half-smile creep in, though it didn't quite reach my eyes. "Hiding from you," I said, trying to keep it light, but the weight behind the words hung between us. She could see right through me, and for a moment, it felt like there was nowhere left to run.

"Hiding from little ol' me?" she teased, grabbing my hand and pulling me closer. Her eyes danced with mine, like we were locked in a chess match; neither of us was quite ready to win. I could feel something between us, a secret she was holding onto, one she seemed ready to let go of.

But I had a secret too—something I'd been carrying for a while, something I wanted to share with her. Yet, even though the moment felt right, I knew it wasn't. Part of me wondered if she'd beat me to it, and I braced myself, hoping she wouldn't suggest something wild, like running around the conference room. That would've been the story of the year—and I definitely wasn't ready to headline that one.

She slowly rose from her chair, her eyes never leaving mine. Each step she took was deliberate and graceful, until she stood directly in front of me. The warmth from her body pulled me in, like gravity. For a split second, all I wanted was to pull her into my arms and kiss her with the same intensity as that day in Dunkin' Donuts. But reality hit hard—she was married, off-limits. How could I even think of sinning against God, against her husband? It felt like I was standing in David's shoes, teetering on the edge of the same mistake he made with Bathsheba.

"I missed you, Naomi," I heard myself say, my convictions thrown out of the window. Just call me pathetic.

"And I missed you, James," she whispered back, her voice soft, full of longing.

Without another thought, we fell into a heartfelt embrace, the kind that went beyond just a simple hug. It was intense, more powerful than anything I'd ever felt. We were in too deep, and both of us knew it.

Holding her felt like nothing I had ever known, her arms draped around my neck, our bodies fitting together as if we were made for this moment. I couldn't help but wonder—how could something that felt so right be so wrong?

"What are we doing?" she breathed, her voice laced with uncertainty as she gently slipped her hands into mine. For a second, it was like we were the only two people in the world, and everything beyond this connection seemed to fade away.

But then, that still, small voice inside me whispered, urging me to look down. And there it was—her diamond ring and wedding band, catching the light like a reminder of everything we were about to cross. The sight of them hit me hard, like a punch to the stomach.

I swallowed hard, pulling my hand from hers, knowing that whatever we thought we wanted, we couldn't let it go any further, not like this.

"What's wrong?" Her fingers brushed my cheek, soft and lingering, like she could feel the shift in me before I could even find the words.

I couldn't stop my eyes from drifting to her hand, where the golden bands circled her finger. My gaze lingered too long, giving me away.

She followed my glance, and, in a barely audible whisper, said, "It's not what you think."

But it didn't matter. I was already stepping back, letting the distance between us grow. "It's cool," I muttered, though the knot in my chest said otherwise. The reality hit me harder than I wanted to admit—she wasn't mine, and deep down, I knew she never would be.

"Give me a chance to explain," she pleaded. "It's really not what you think. We're not—"

Before she could finish, the conference room doors swung open. A stream of guests began filling the room, their conversations buzzing and drowning out the quiet between us. Without saying another word, I turned and walked away from Naomi. Each step toward the front of the room felt like dragging a weight, my mind a tangled mess of 'what ifs' that would never be.

As I glanced back, I saw her standing by the exit, a polite smile on her lips as she spoke with the guests. But beneath the calm, I could see the storm raging inside her. When our eyes met, she mouthed the words that both healed and shattered me: "I love you."

I wanted to return the sentiment, to tell her I felt the same, but the truth crashed down hard: Naomi didn't belong to me. She was tied to someone else, and no matter how much I longed for her, that reality was inescapable. Still, she had unknowingly claimed my heart, and in my mind, it was hers alone. Her silent confession confirmed what we both knew but could never act on. It would be our secret, buried deep—maybe forever—waiting for a moment that might never come.

I tried to clear my head, knowing that dwelling on what could never be would only make things harder. The president of the company walked on stage and tapped the microphone. "Testing, one, two, three. Testing, one, two, three," she said, snapping me back to the present. It was my cue to focus on why I was there, though my heart was still tangled in everything Naomi stirred in me.

I took my seat in the front row, watching the event unfold. The president, full of charm, kicked off the day with some light-hearted jokes that drew easy laughter from the crowd. The atmosphere was warm and relaxed, but my mind couldn't escape Naomi. Her quiet, calming presence only intensified the emotional storm raging inside me.

As the time came to introduce the first speaker, Naomi's elegance commanded the room. The president's voice echoed, "Our first speaker is from Richmond, Virginia. She is the leader of one of the fastest-growing churches in the country. Please join me in welcoming Pastor Naomi Adams."

The crowd stood in unison, applause filling the space as Naomi moved gracefully down the aisle. Each step she took radiated confidence, her poise unmistakable. Her smile lit up the room, effortlessly connecting with everyone she passed. But when she reached me, her gaze held mine, and in that fleeting, silent moment, everything else disappeared. The pull between us was undeniable, an unspoken truth that we belonged together—even if the universe had other plans.

# CHAPTER 13



THE DAY HAD DRAGGED ON, EVEN WITH THE STANDING ovation I got after my speech on letting go of the unknown and embracing the new. I should've been riding high, especially since Naomi gave me a shout-out at the end of her speech, just before I took the stage. It was subtle, but I knew what it meant. A smooth move by her—the same woman who knew I wanted her, slipping in that little nod in front of everyone. It felt good, but it also left me uneasy, as if she was playing some game that only the two of us understood.

Once the event wrapped up, I was ready to get out of there faster than an inmate on early release. Forget the usual pleasantries—the handshakes, the "thanks for coming" or "great to meet you" routine. But habit took over. I smiled, shook hands, and passed out business cards to corporate bigwigs eager to book me for their next event.

Naomi was across the room, surrounded by a group of women, laughing and chatting, when I decided to make my exit. I slipped toward the door, trying to go unnoticed. But of course, she spotted me. I saw her hand shoot up, probably ready to flag me down. My heart pounded as I pretended not to see, slipping out of the room just before she could chase me down. I couldn't help but picture her running after me through the hotel lobby—that would've been a scene for sure.

Inside my room, I could barely think straight. My hands were trembling as I crammed everything into my bag—shirts wrinkling, shoes landing in a heap. I fumbled with my suitcase, my hands trembling as I stuffed clothes inside. Every creak in the hallway made my heart race—I could almost feel Naomi's knock before it came. The room seemed to shrink with each passing second, the air heavy with the tension I couldn't shake. After a quick scan to make sure I hadn't left anything behind, I grabbed my bag and rushed to the door.

Instead of the elevator, I made a beeline for the stairs, taking them two at a time like I was training for a marathon. No way Naomi would think to check here—she wasn't exactly the stair-taking type. I reached the bottom, shoved the door open, ready to taste freedom—until I looked up.

There she was, standing right there, like she'd known exactly where to find me.

Caught off guard, I stammered, "Hey! I was just... uh, looking for you."

She crossed her arms, one eyebrow arched. "In the stairwell? Really?"

# CHAPTER 14

*A real friend sticks closer than a brother*

AS I TRIED TO SNEAK OUT OF THE HOTEL WITHOUT saying goodbye to Naomi, I felt like a kid caught with cookie crumbs all over his face. Plan A had crashed and burned, leaving me scrambling to activate Plan B—which, if all went well, would kick in right about... *now.*

Riiiinnnnggg! Right on cue. I fished my phone out of my jacket and practically shouted, "YES!"—like it was a winning lottery ticket. Maybe I was a bit too loud, but I didn't care. Perfect timing. "You're a lifesaver," I muttered under my breath, grinning like a fool as if the phone had solved all my problems.

I held up the phone toward Naomi to prove I was on a call as we walked into the lobby. "Naomi, this is my friend Will. Will, meet Naomi."

Will, loud as ever, shouted, "Good Lord, she's beautiful! Holy Mother of Jesus, turn that phone back around! I need another look at her. No way a woman that gorgeous is a pastor!"

I glanced at Naomi, who was clearly trying not to laugh. "Sorry about that," I mumbled. "He's got a one-track mind."

Will's voice boomed again, "And that track's name is *Hotness Overload!*"

I turned to Naomi, with a sense of embarrassment and disbelief, "Well, that's one way to get introduced."

Slipping her arm under mine, Naomi gently pulled me toward the hotel restaurant. I tried to manage a smile, but I was sweating bullets.

As we settled into seats at the bar, Will's voice blared through the phone once more. "Bro, are you out of your mind trying to dodge a woman who's hotter than Megan Good and serves the Lord? That's like winning the lottery twice!"

I chuckled nervously, trying to regain my composure. "But what about the Knicks game tonight? Didn't you say you had courtside seats?"

I was desperate to steer Will back to the plan—anything to get me out of this tight spot. I glanced at Naomi, who was watching me with a raised eyebrow and a smirk that suggested she knew exactly what was going on. Her calm, knowing look only made me sweat more, like she could see straight into my panicked mind.

Will's laughter rang through the phone, completely unfazed by my predicament. "Oh, that's why I was calling! I'm taking my wife instead."

"What?" I gritted my teeth, whispering under my breath. "You no-good mother—" My words came out in a barely audible growl. With friends like Will, who needed enemies? He was supposed to bail me out, not toss me under the bus.

Naomi's gaze was locked on me now, her lips curling into a slight smile as if to say, *really?* I could feel the heat rising in my face, my plan crumbling right in front of me.

"Enjoy your evening, loverboy," Will laughed, hanging up before I could say a word.

I stood there, phone still in my hand, stunned. Naomi had clearly heard everything. She leaned back, arms crossed, an amused smirk on her face.

"Well," she said, holding back a laugh, "looks like your plans just changed."

I let out an awkward laugh, shoving my phone into my pocket. "Yeah, guess dinner's back on the table."

Naomi just shook her head, clearly entertained by my failed escape. "Running off like that? And with a wingman like him? You've got no chance."

I grinned. *Guess it's all on me now.*

# CHAPTER 15



WILL WAS RIGHT ABOUT ONE THING: NAOMI WAS ONE of the most stunning women I'd ever met. Despite the magnetic pull I felt toward her, I knew we could only be friends, though even that felt like navigating a slippery slope. One minute, I wanted to run from her like Joseph fleeing from Potiphar's wife, and the next, I was imagining all sorts of things a single man should never even consider about a married woman.

Just then, the bartender, a tall, burly guy with piercing blue eyes, approached us. He set down two coasters with a thud, giving us a friendly smile. "What can I get you two tonight?"

His smile felt like it was mocking my internal struggle. As if sensing the tension, he added, "And I promise, no one's going to judge you here for your choices. I've seen it all."

I forced a laugh, hoping to deflect the awkwardness, while Naomi's calm demeanor only added to my mounting anxiety.

He looked at me, then Naomi, then back to me again, his gaze almost comically exaggerated. I gave a slight nod to Naomi, which she took as my subtle way of saying "ladies first."

With a graceful smile, she turned to the bartender. "I'll have a virgin Strawberry Daiquiri and a bottle of FIJI water."

"Nice choice," he said, glancing at me with a look that seemed to say, *You can do better than that.*

Feeling the pressure and knowing I needed something strong to get through the evening, I blurted out, "I'll have a double shot of bourbon and no water."

He gave me a knowing look, like he approved. "Coming right up," he said with a nod.

As he walked away, I let out a heavy sigh. Thoughts of her swirled in my head, twisting into something I couldn't explain—or justify. I glanced at the ceiling, half-expecting God to be watching, shaking His head. It felt like standing under a spotlight in a room full of mirrors—no way to hide, no excuses. My grip tightened on the edge of the bar. A stiff drink wouldn't fix this.

# CHAPTER 16



"A VIRGIN STRAWBERRY DAIQUIRI AND A BOTTLE OF FIJI water for the lady, and a double shot of bourbon for the guy in the expensive suit," the bartender announced with a half-hearted joke. But his words barely reached me. Inside, I was wrestling with a storm of conflicting desires. The more time I spent with Naomi, the more I felt the pull of temptation, knowing full well she was married.

I could already feel it—the shift from lighthearted laughter to something heavier, something I shouldn't even be considering. I caught myself leaning in a little too close, laughing a little too loud. Each second that passed, each smile I returned, had me inching closer to a line I'd promised myself I wouldn't cross.

"Thanks," I managed, slipping him a hundred-dollar bill, hoping the gesture would help me escape the moral quicksand I was sinking into.

His eyes lit up as he pocketed the bill like it was a winning lottery ticket. "No, thank you!" he said, almost too eagerly. "If you need anything, just holler."

As I took my drink and tried to steady my nerves, the truth sank in: I was fighting more than just the allure of Naomi. I was battling my own sense of right and wrong, and the longer I stayed, the harder it would be to walk away unscathed.

"Bartender," I called out, tapping the shot glass, bracing for round two.

In a heartbeat, he appeared with another shot. "This one's on the house," he winked. "But do me a favor—keep it between us. My boss would kill me."

"Your secret's safe," I replied, though my insides churned. This wasn't about the drink. It was about silencing the voice that screamed I was headed for disaster.

I glanced at Naomi, and for a split second, it felt like the air between us was charged, heavy with what we both knew but hadn't said. Her gaze lingered, and I could feel that pull, like gravity, tugging me closer. My heart raced, and my pulse picked up. If I didn't take a step back right now, I knew I'd be trapped, crossing a line I'd never be able to undo. The bourbon wouldn't be enough to drown it out, and I was running out of excuses to put space between us.

"You're not driving, right?" Naomi's voice broke through my thoughts as she snatched the glass from my hand. Before I could answer, she slipped off the barstool and walked over to the bartender. My heart sank as I watched her lean in, pointing back at me like I'd committed some unforgivable act.

Ol' blue eyes gave me a knowing glance, then nodded at her request.

When she returned, she slid onto her stool with a knowing smile, placing the glass just out of my reach. "No more drinks for you."

I blinked, stunned. "Did you just—?"

"Yep," she interrupted, smirking. "Had to cut you off before you confessed something you can't take back."

My chest tightened. She had no idea how hard I was fighting to keep the truth inside—that this pull between us was a dangerous game I shouldn't be playing. The more time I spent with her, the closer I got to betraying everything I believed in. And it wasn't just the drinks. It was the way I *wanted* her. A kind of wanting that I knew was wrong in God's eyes, in her husband's eyes... and in my own.

# CHAPTER 17

## Lean not on your own understanding

SUNDAY MORNING STRETCHED ON, SLOWER THAN I'D hoped. I pulled myself out of bed, feeling the effects of last night's game. The Celtics had won, but all I could feel was the headache and the exhaustion. I shuffled into the kitchen, barefoot on the cold tile, and eyed the Peet's coffee pod, hoping it would be strong enough to get the day started.

I popped the pod into the Keurig, the sound of brewing coffee filling the quiet kitchen. While I waited, I wandered back to the bedroom and grabbed my phone from the nightstand.

Once the coffee was ready, I wrapped my hands around the warm mug and made my way into the living room. I turned on the TV to SportsCenter, then dropped onto the couch, feeling the cold leather shift under me as I sank in. I took a slow sip, letting the heat hit my throat, trying to shake off the last bit of sleep.

Then, just as I set my phone down on the coffee table, the screen lit up. I glanced over, puzzled. It was barely 7:30 in the morning. Who on earth could be messaging me this early?

As soon as I saw Naomi's name on the screen, my stomach dropped. I hesitated, my finger hovering over the unlock button. Whatever was waiting for me behind that screen was bound to throw my peaceful Sunday morning off course.

Hey stranger, it's me, Naomi.

Just reading her words was like opening a door I wasn't sure I wanted to walk through. I took a long sip of coffee, but even the bitterness couldn't steady the unease tightening in my chest.

It was great seeing you at the event last month, and your speech was excellent. I even had one of my assistants record it.

Wait, she'd recorded it? Without me even knowing? I wasn't sure whether to be flattered or freaked out.

I wanted to share it with you while we were at the bar, but your sudden departure made me realize I'd have to wait until we crossed paths again.

Of course, she noticed my sudden exit. I should've known better—Naomi wasn't the type to let anything slip past her.

> Well, today, I'm preaching at the church, and I'm inviting you out as my special guest. Service starts at 10:00 am sharp. I look forward to seeing you, and maybe afterward, we can grab a bite to eat.

I let out a low whistle. Preaching at church and then lunch? There was no way this was going to stay casual. Naomi was always smooth like that—slipping in an invitation that sounded innocent, but I knew better.

> Well, before I write you a novel, I'll end it here. See you soon, James. Ciao! Oh, and in case you don't remember the address of the church, here it is.

I stared at the message, the reality of it sinking in. I hadn't been to church in months—and honestly, I wasn't even sure I wanted to start now. But there was something about Naomi. She had a way of drawing me in without even trying, like a gravitational force I couldn't escape, no matter how much I tried.

Two hours later, I found myself standing by the front door, sharply dressed, Bible in one hand, keys in the other, shaking my head at the situation I'd walked into. *The power of an influential woman is a dangerous thing,* I thought, chuckling to myself as I stepped outside. The crisp morning air hit me, but it wasn't enough to clear the mess in my head.

I knew I was playing with fire, heading to Naomi's church like this. It wasn't just a casual Sunday service; it felt like stepping into something deeper, something I wasn't sure I was ready for. But here I was, walking to my truck like a man with no other choice. Naomi had that kind of pull. She'd invite you to something simple, but you always sensed there was more beneath the surface, and that's what had me on edge.

*You're walking into a fire,* I thought again, gripping the steering wheel tighter as I started the engine.

It was 10:05 a.m. when I pulled into the church parking lot, my head on a swivel, hoping the service had already started. The lot was packed, but I spotted a few stragglers making their way toward the entrance, probably latecomers like me. I found a spot in the back, turned off the engine, and leaned my seat back as far as it would go. I needed to wait for the coast to clear before heading in. *What am I doing here?* I thought. *Am I a glutton for punishment? Or worse, about to be roped into some kind of spiritual marathon?*

I couldn't believe I'd actually come. Was I walking straight into trouble, or was this my twisted way of seeking redemption? The last thing I needed was a surprise encounter with Naomi's husband or, even worse, Sam. If I ran into him, I might have to imagine the whole "Stomp" routine from Kirk Franklin playing in the background while I made my getaway.

I let out a deep breath, glancing at the clock on my dashboard. 10:15 a.m. The service was surely in full swing by now. Hoping the congregation was in the middle of *Amazing Grace* or one of those long worship medleys, I hopped out of the truck. Tip-toeing toward the entrance, I prayed that everyone was too focused on their praise to notice me sneaking in. The last thing I needed was to draw any attention.

As I walked into the church, my focus was solely on Naomi—a married woman who had taken hold of my heart in ways I wasn't ready to admit. But the moment I stepped into the empty lobby, my conscience hit me like a runaway freight train. Before I knew it, I was on my knees, praying like I was auditioning for a role in a dramatic movie scene.

"God, I've messed up," I started, feeling like I'd stumbled into the script of a melodrama. "Here I am, in your house, where I should be worshiping you, but instead, my heart's gone completely off track. It's tangled up in thoughts of Naomi—your servant, no less. She's all I think about, even in my sleep. I wake up half expecting to find myself in one of those cheesy rom-coms where she's the leading lady who's always just out of reach. And her husband? He's done nothing wrong, yet here I am, betraying him in my mind. I'm ashamed, Lord. Truly ashamed."

I took a deep breath, forcing myself to focus. "Lord, I think I love her. My thoughts are a mess—impure, dangerous, and honestly, they're borderline criminal. I don't even know how I got here, but I'm begging you—please, take this desire away from me. Free my heart and my mind from this woman who's already made a vow to someone else. These feelings are eating me alive, and every time I try to do right, it feels like evil's right there, laughing in my face. I need you, Lord. You're the reason I'm here today. You're my strength, my guide, and I give you all the honor and glory. Help me not to sin against you or your people—not here, not anywhere. Amen."

When I opened my eyes, Naomi was standing right there, her hand gently resting on my shoulder. I hadn't noticed her approach, but now I felt the warmth of her touch, and her hand trembled slightly—like she wanted to offer comfort but wasn't sure how.

"Did you hear everything I prayed?" I asked, my voice shaky. My heart was still racing from the prayer.

She nodded, slow and deliberate, holding my gaze like she could see straight through me. Then, in a voice so soft I almost missed it, she said, "Me too."

Then she turned and walked back toward the inner part of the church. The door clicked softly as it closed behind her, leaving me alone in the lobby, the silence heavy with what had just passed between us.

I stood up, my head still spinning from the emotional rollercoaster. As I glanced toward the door, my heart skipped. An angry man stormed toward me, his face twisted in fury, fist clenched tight. My first thought was, *Is this Naomi's husband, ready to throw down right here in the church?*

My imagination went wild—fighting in the church, dealing with a jealous husband, all because of my unchecked feelings. I could almost see the headlines: "Man Brawls Over Unrequited Love in Sacred Space." My stomach twisted at the thought.

The man reached me, and just as I braced for a confrontation, he blurted out, "Do you know where the men's bathroom is?" His intense look was all about his urgent need, not a tussle in the House of the Lord.

Relief washed over me, and I couldn't help but laugh at my overactive imagination. I pointed him in the right direction, though my hands were still a bit shaky from the scare.

As the man hurried off, I let out a deep breath, my heart still racing. The thought of almost having to throw punches in the House of the Lord seemed ridiculous now, and a nervous laugh rose up inside me. Shaking off the stress, I stepped into the inner sanctuary for the first time, unsure of what I'd find.

The air felt different in here—heavier, like it carried the weight of everyone's prayers. I slipped into a seat at the very back, close to the exit, just in case I had to make a mad dash out. The choir had already started, their voices rising up together in a song I didn't recognize.

Suddenly, out of the corner of my eye, I saw Sam. I hadn't seen him since that awkward day at Dunkin Donuts. He stood up, turned, and started making a beeline straight for me, eyes locked on like a heat-seeking missile. My stomach dropped. I swallowed hard, silently praying he was just heading to the bathroom, like the other guy. But nope, just my luck; he stopped right in front of me, grinning like he'd found a long-lost friend.

"Brother James!" he said, slapping a hand on my shoulder with way too much excitement. "What are you doing all the way back here in the nosebleed section? Come on up front!"

"My nose isn't bleeding," I joked, hoping to lighten the mood, but Sam wasn't biting. He just smiled wider, and that's when he dropped the bomb.

"Pastor Naomi sent me to come get you," he said, extending his hand like this was the most normal thing in the world.

"Said you're her special guest. And you know Pastor Naomi—she doesn't take no for an answer."

I sighed, like I was about to sink into the pew. Of course. No getting out of this now. I grabbed my Bible and stood up, feeling like I was walking to my doom. I followed Sam down the aisle, keeping a calm face, but inside, I was shouting, *Why me? Why now?* My feet kept moving, but in my head, I was already halfway to the parking lot.

# CHAPTER 18

## *The gift of the Holy Spirit*

"FASTEN YOUR SEATBELT, YOUNG MAN," AN ELDERLY gentleman to my left said, slapping the back of my neck with surprising force. I jumped a little, caught off guard. He leaned in, a grin spreading across his face. "Pastor's about to preach a word that's gonna set the house on fire!"

I forced a smile, rubbing the back of my neck where his hand had landed. *Seatbelt?* I thought. If this sermon was anything like what Sam had just put me through, I might need a full-blown harness.

*On fire?* I glanced to my left, where a mini fire extinguisher was mounted less than fifty feet away. *Well, if things did heat up, at least I'd have a shot at saving myself and Naomi.* I wasn't exactly sure what the old man meant, but I wasn't about to take any chances.

"Yes, the word is about to be delivered," a voice chimed in, pulling my attention. I turned to see a beautiful dark-skinned woman with curly black hair and a short black dress that hugged her toned thighs. *Seriously?* I thought. *How am I supposed to focus now?* Of all the seats in the church, I had to end up next to temptation itself, right in the house of the Lord.

I knew one thing for sure—if I didn't get these wandering eyes under control immediately, the Lord Himself might have to come down from heaven and give me a personal rebuke. The struggle was very, very real.

"Well, I guess I better hurry up and fasten my seatbelt before some of the pastor's fiery sermon burns the house down around me," I joked, chuckling to myself. But the old man just stared at me, stone-faced, like I'd just said something completely out of line. *Hold on,* I thought. *He's the one who said the pastor was going to set the place on fire, not me!*

He rubbed his chin, eyes still locked on me in a way that made my skin crawl. His gaze lingered far too long, and I had half a mind to tell him to stop staring, to mind his own business. But instead, I clenched my jaw and turned my attention to the stage, doing my best to shake off the awkwardness.

On stage, a short, bald man in an oversized suit emerged from behind the curtain. He gave the crowd a wide smile and a wave, like he was some kind of celebrity. Then he casually removed the small microphone from the podium at the center of the stage, clearly gearing up for something big. I couldn't help but think, *This is the guy who's going to set the house on fire?*

"Good morning, church," his deep baritone voice boomed through the auditorium, commanding everyone's attention—even the old man next to me finally quit staring and turned to face the stage. "God is good, and His faithfulness endures forever."

"Praise the Lord!" a woman's voice called out behind me. "Praise Your holy name!"

The preacher raised his left arm high, voice rising with it. "God is good!" he shouted.

"All the time…" the whole room responded in unison.

"And all the time," he wailed.

"God is good!" they all shouted back, loud and proud.

I sat there, silent, glancing around like I'd missed a cue in a play. Apparently, this was something the Black church was known for—a call-and-response.

I must have missed the memo, because while everyone else was in sync, I was sitting there feeling like the odd one out.

After delivering the morning announcements and welcoming all the first-time visitors, the preacher offered a quick prayer, then walked off the stage so smoothly it was like he had never been there at all. Just like that, the energy shifted.

Seconds later, the curtain opened, revealing the choir, heads bowed. The guitarist and drummer were already bobbing their heads along with the quiet rhythm, waiting for the cue. Then, the keyboardist started playing—soft, delicate notes, as beautiful as birdsong at dawn. It was the kind of melody that made your heart slow down and your mind go quiet.

Before I knew it, my foot was tapping along, completely on its own. And then, she appeared—Naomi. She stepped forward, her eyes brimming with tears, catching the light in a way that made them sparkle. Just seeing her like that hit me hard, a mix of emotions rising up in my chest that I couldn't even begin to name.

"I sought the Lord, and He heard and He answered," Naomi sang, her voice strong and steady. The congregation stood, joining in, but her eyes stayed locked on mine.

I couldn't look away. It felt like she was singing just for me. Each tear that rolled down her face felt like it carried something sacred, something I didn't deserve to hold, but still, I wanted to.

Then, in a surreal moment, she descended the steps, never breaking eye contact. Her voice carried through the room, but it felt like a private concert meant only for the two of us. My heart pounded, but I couldn't look away. Slowly, my hands lifted in surrender as I joined in, my voice blending with the chorus of the congregation.

"I trust in God, my Savior. He will never fail," I sang, the words spilling out like a confession. And then, without warning, Naomi's hand found mine—soft, steady, and impossibly warm.

Before I knew it, she was leading me up onto the stage with the choir. I was singing right along with them, not with the grace of a bird but more like a rooster at sunrise. Yet, for that moment, it didn't matter. There I was, in front of the entire church, standing next to Naomi, and feeling something I couldn't quite describe.

For the first time since Naomi had invited me to church, I felt… whole. Maybe it was the warmth of her hand in mine, the connection we shared in front of the entire congregation, or the way the moment felt almost sacred. It was like everything had aligned just right, and for a split second, I believed this moment was priceless.

Something tugged at me, a quiet whisper I couldn't ignore. As perfect as this felt—her hand in mine, the music surrounding us—there was a voice in my head: *This isn't what it seems.* I wanted this, wanted her, but I couldn't shake the feeling that it wasn't meant to be.

I gripped her hand tighter, the question burning in my mind: *God, is this you?* Why did this feel so right if it wasn't? Why did she feel like everything I've ever wanted?

But the guilt wouldn't let go. *I know this isn't your plan. I know I've messed up. But if it's not right, why does it feel impossible to stop?*

It was like standing on the edge of something I couldn't undo. The weight of the choice pressed down on me, making it hard to breathe. If I crossed this line, there was no going back.

Naomi leaned in closer, her voice low but steady. "I need you to trust me. Do you?"

Her words hit me like a punch I didn't see coming. My throat went dry. Trust her? I didn't even trust myself right now. Right then, I knew—nothing would ever be the same.

# CHAPTER 19



AS THE MEDLEY ENDED, I MADE MY WAY BACK TO MY seat, and there he was—the old man, waiting for me with open arms. The grin on his face made it clear I was no longer a stranger in his eyes. "Come here, son," he said, pulling me into a hug that felt more like a father embracing his son than a churchgoer greeting someone he barely knew.

Something in me softened. I felt like I belonged, like I wasn't just there for Naomi anymore. Wiping a single tear from my eye with the back of my hand, I realized something inside me was shifting. I didn't know what it was, but there was no denying it— the presence of God was near, closer than I'd ever felt before.

With my head bowed, I felt my eyes start to well up again. *What is happening to me?* I hadn't cried in over ten years. But here I was, tearing up in front of a room full of strangers, feeling exposed in a way I hadn't allowed myself to be in years. "Get it together," I muttered under my breath, but I'm sure those around me heard it.

Then I felt it—a soft touch on my leg. Gentle, almost hesitant. It was definitely a woman's hand. I glanced over and saw the woman in the black dress, her hand resting on me as she rocked back and forth in her seat, praying in a language I didn't recognize. My first instinct was to pull away, to snap back into control, but something stopped me.

Instead, I closed my eyes and began praying, too, pouring everything out with such passion that everything else around me seemed to disappear. The room went silent. It was like I was suddenly alone, just me and God.

Somehow, I found myself on my knees, tears streaming down my face. Naomi and a handful of others were standing around me, their hands on my shoulders, on my back, praying for me with a force I couldn't explain. It felt like a dream—too surreal to be real. But it was happening. I could feel it.

The presence of God was so thick, so powerful, it was almost overwhelming. I knew in my heart something was shifting, that real change was coming. And then, in the silence, I heard it.

*Protect your mind.* The words rang out clearly, echoing over and over in my head. It wasn't just a thought. I knew it was God speaking. *Protect your mind, my chosen vessel, and come to the altar. I hear you, son.*

And then, just like that, the voice was gone. But its weight lingered in my heart, like an undeniable truth I couldn't ignore.

When I opened my eyes, I was back in my seat. The choir was on stage, singing with the same fervor as before, and the old man and the woman in the black dress were swaying gently to the music, as if nothing had happened.

*Wait, what just happened?* I blinked, trying to piece together the confusion swirling in my head. Was that all just a dream? Or was Jesus calling me in a way I couldn't fully grasp?

The warmth and intensity of the moment felt real, but now everything seemed so ordinary, so normal. My heart raced as I tried to make sense of the experience. It was like waking up from a dream where you're still trying to catch your breath, unsure if what you felt was truly real.

# CHAPTER 20

*Even in the darkness I cannot hide*

FOR THE NEXT HOUR AND A HALF, I STAYED GLUED TO my seat, wrestling with my thoughts. Had I dozed off and dreamed the whole thing, or had God really shown up in some kind of vision, just for me? What made me so special that the Almighty Himself would make an appearance?

The altar call started. People were getting up, walking to the front, making their public commitments to God. I felt the pull, sharp and insistent, like someone had grabbed my collar and was dragging me forward.

But I didn't move.

I already had a relationship with God... right? That was enough. It had to be.

So, I stayed where I was, gripping the edge of the pew like it might anchor me. My thoughts swirled. My heart raced. The clock ticked. I just wanted the service to end.

After the service, I headed straight for the exit, weaving through the crowd like a man on a mission. The last thing I needed was to get cornered by an overly friendly church member eager to sign me up for something. I wasn't about to stick around for a sales pitch disguised as salvation.

As soon as I stepped into the lobby, there he was—the old man from earlier. He was deep in conversation with a woman in a giant red hat, but his eyes kept darting over her shoulder, locking onto me. He was waving, clearly trying to get my attention.

I ignored him, keeping my head down and my pace steady. The exit was in sight. Almost there.

Once I was outside, a rush of relief hit me, and I couldn't help but mutter under my breath, "Free at last, thank God Almighty, I'm free at last." I even considered breaking into a jog, but as I reached my car, a familiar voice stopped me cold.

"Brother James?"

I turned around to see Sam, along with a few other well-dressed older gentlemen, making their way toward me. *Why me?* I thought, forcing a fake smile. There was no escape now.

"Where are you running off to so soon?" Sam called out, glancing at the other guys with him. "We're about to have a fellowship lunch, and we'd love for you to join us. I don't know if the pastor mentioned it, but today is *Family and Friends Day*. You're more than just a friend—you're practically family!"

Family? I wasn't sure I could even call them distant cousins, let alone relatives. Still, they nudged me back toward the church, steering me inside like I had no say in the matter.

"So, how did you enjoy today's service?" one of the guys asked. He was tall and wiry, with long cornrows that seemed to sway with his movements. I shrugged, unsure how to sum up the whirlwind of emotions I'd just experienced.

"It was a nice service," I said, keeping it short. Small talk wasn't really my thing. All I wanted was to get home, crack open a beer, and catch the New England Patriots game. It was already 3 o'clock, and kickoff was at 4. I'd been here for nearly five hours. What was it with black churches and their marathon services?

"Well, this will be your chance to meet some great brothers and sisters," Sam said, throwing his arm around my neck and pulling me closer.

*Loosen your grip before I suplex you,* I thought, feeling a surge of frustration bubbling up, not from the Holy Spirit, but from sheer annoyance. Then, my mind drifted back to the woman in the black dress. As I was about to ask about her, I noticed her standing next to a tall, muscular guy with tattoos on his neck and three teardrop tattoos under his eye. It didn't take much to guess—he was probably her man.

What was it with me and attracting women who were already taken? I shook my head and followed the group into a large room. Tables were set up in the middle, surrounded by chairs, and a buffet stretched across the far side. Naomi walked in shortly after, her eyes scanning the crowd.

When our eyes met, it felt like she was giving me that unmistakable look—the kind that says, *I want you, but I can't have you right now.* Or maybe that was the look I was giving her. Either way, she made her way over to me, slipped her arm under mine, and guided me to the front of the food line.

"We need to talk about that prayer—or rather, that confession you were having with God before the service started," Naomi said, her voice firm but gentle.

Before I could respond, a group of stunning women surrounded us, their beauty making me feel like I'd stumbled into a fashion show rather than a church function. They circled around me, making me feel like the evening's main attraction. I'd never seen so many gorgeous women in one place.

"Ladies," Naomi said, her arm linked with mine as she pulled me in a little closer. "This is James Barnes, all the way from Boston. James, meet my beautiful sisters in Christ."

"Nice to meet you, Brother James," they said, all smiles. One of them squeezed my hand like we were old friends, and before I knew it, a phone number slipped into my palm. "Call me," she said with a wink, like she'd done this a hundred times before

After the introductions, we were treated to a spread: baked chicken, collard greens, macaroni and cheese, and chocolate cake. Naomi and I grabbed a table, but my mind couldn't stop circling back to one question—*where was her husband?* He had to be around here somewhere. I scanned the room and spotted a few sharp-dressed men, their glares colder than a winter morning. *Could one of them be the guy I'd have to answer to?*

# CHAPTER 21

*Come to me, all who are weary*

THE DOOR CREAKED AS I PUSHED IT OPEN, AND I leaned heavily against the frame, taking a deep breath. The clock on the wall read 4:10 p.m., but it felt like midnight. My whole body ached, not from any physical exertion, but from the kind of mental and emotional drain only five hours of church can pull off. I didn't walk into the apartment so much as I *collapsed* into it, as my legs could barely carry me another step. The suit jacket slid off my shoulders and hit the floor in a heap, but I didn't even care. Five hours. *How did I survive that?*

I stood there for a second, staring blankly at the room. No chance I could do this every Sunday. The thought of being glued to a pew for that long, week after week, made me shiver. Maybe Easter and Christmas weren't such bad options after all, especially with football season in full swing. The smell of my stale cologne mixed with exhaustion made my decision feel more certain. *Yeah, I'm not cut out for this.*

At least I'd planned ahead. DVR set, phone off—no chance I was letting ESPN ruin the scores for me. I yanked off my tie and the rest of my Sunday best, grabbed my favorite sweats, and headed for the fridge. One cold Corona later, I flopped onto the couch like it was the only thing that could save me. It was late, sure. But the day wasn't over yet. Not completely.

The Patriots were playing the Browns, so it wasn't exactly going to be a nail-biter. I propped my feet up on the coffee table and downed my first beer like it was water. By the second, I could feel my eyes getting heavier, the long day catching up to me. With the Pats already up 17-0 by the end of the first quarter, I figured, why not watch the rest from bed? Bad idea. My head barely hit the pillow before I was out cold. Game over—for me, at least.

When I opened my eyes, the clock on the bedside table read 10:43 p.m. I groaned, realizing I'd missed three-quarters of the game. Still, my spirits lifted as I flicked on the NFL app and saw the final score: Patriots 27, Browns 13. The GOAT, Tom Brady, had worked his magic again—259 passing yards, two touchdowns, and another win to add to his undefeated streak. And Coach Belichick? He'd just racked up his 300th career victory. I couldn't have asked for a better way to end the day.

But it wasn't just the win that had me smiling. I was $500 richer. Will had bet against the Patriots. He'd actually thought the Pats wouldn't cover a ten-point spread and that Baker Mayfield was somehow going to tear through our defense like he was Tom Brady's long-lost twin. I couldn't wait to call him up and rub it in. Maybe I'd start singing Another One Bites the Dust right when he picked up, just to hear him try to explain himself. Will hated losing, and I was about to make sure he felt every bit of it.

I jumped out of bed, panic creeping in when I realized my phone was nowhere to be found. I scrambled around, yanking my suit from the dry cleaner's bag, tearing through it like I was searching for treasure. No phone. Did I leave it in the car?

I slipped into my Retro Jordans, grabbed my keys, and was about to head out when I caught sight of it on the coffee table. There it was, resting next to the empty Corona bottles.

I let out a relieved sigh and dropped my keys back into the basket by the door. The panic melted away, replaced by a kid-like excitement as I skipped into the living room, already imagining how I'd spend my winnings.

As the phone screen lit up, I couldn't fight the grin that spread across my face. With both Cash App and Venmo on his phone, Will had no excuse not to pay up. But then my smile vanished. Seven missed calls. Nine text messages. All from *Naomi*.

# CHAPTER 22



I STARED AT THE PHONE SCREEN FOR A FEW MINUTES, feeling like I was drowning in a sea of missed calls and texts. Each notification felt like it was shouting at me. Taking a deep breath, I braced myself and finally tapped on the first message.

Hey Mr. Disappearing Act. What's with you always vanishing before we have a serious chat? I'm starting to think you're deliberately avoiding me. But anyway, it was nice seeing you at church today. I was really surprised to see you up on stage singing—though my advice is, don't quit your day job. Lol. When you get this, give me a call. I'm out with a few friends, so don't worry about disturbing me. Looking forward to catching up. Ciao!

The message wasn't as harsh as I'd feared. Maybe I was just overreacting. Feeling a bit more at ease, I decided to move on to the next message.

Must be a pretty good game. I tried calling earlier to see if you wanted to join me for dinner later, but I only got your voicemail. Call me when you get a chance.

I braced myself for the third message, my palms sweating as I scrolled.

I don't want you to think I'm stalking you, but my friends have been pestering me about you all afternoon. They keep saying you're very handsome. What do you do again? Just kidding. We're still at the restaurant. Call me when you're free. I hope you're enjoying the game. Call me.

A warning bell went off in my head as I moved to the next message. I hesitated but ignored the feeling and read it.

I've left you four messages in less than an hour. I'm not in the habit of harassing people or leaving this many messages, but that must be one heck of a game, or maybe you have company. If that's the case, forgive me for interrupting.

As I read through the fifth, sixth, and seventh texts, my unease grew. The persistence was starting to cross into creepy territory. By the time I reached the eighth message, a chill ran down my spine. This wasn't just weird—it was downright unsettling. Despite every urge to delete the messages and block her number, my stubborn ego kept me scrolling.

> This is my eighth message, and I'm starting to worry about you.
> I've called you more times than I should have. Please call me
> back. I just want to make sure you're okay.

I gulped, bracing myself as I moved to the final message, expecting the worst. When I read it, I couldn't help but chuckle, though my amusement was mixed with a hint of panic.

> Brother James, this is my last and final message to you. I've
> called the hospitals and even the police station, and no
> one by your name has been admitted or arrested. Thank God.
> Since you're too busy to pick up your phone, I'm going to pay
> you a surprise visit. Oh, and I got your address from the welcome card you filled out when you first visited the church. I'll
> see you soon. And you better answer the door.

I froze, shocked and confused. What was happening? The whole thing felt like some twisted joke. But if there was a punchline, I had a sinking feeling I wasn't going to like it.

No way this could be happening. My mind raced, my face starting to sweat, heart pounding in my chest. What in the name of Mary, the mother of Jesus, was going on? I'd planned to call Will later to collect my $500, but right now, all I could think about was the simple—yet completely unexpected—possibility that Naomi was actually on her way to my apartment. Of all the things I could be dealing with right now, this was definitely not one of them.

The thought of a married woman showing up at a single guy's place after 11 p.m. felt completely off. My stomach twisted as I tried to wrap my head around it. There was no way she was serious about this, right?

With no other options, I sank onto the couch and decided to pray. It was my last shot at avoiding what could turn into a disaster. I clasped my hands together, doing my best to ignore the sweat gathering in my palms, and whispered the most desperate prayer I'd ever said.

"God, I don't know what's happening or why Naomi decided to come to my place. Please, I don't want anything bad to happen to her—not even a flat tire on the way over. And if you could, maybe keep her away from my place entirely? In Jesus' name, I pray, amen. Oh, and one more thing—I didn't really mean what I said about only coming to church for Easter and Christmas. Just a bad joke, I promise!"

As I finished, I couldn't help but laugh at how ridiculous this all seemed. Here I was, staring at the door like Naomi was about to burst through it any second. The suspense was almost too much, and every sound outside had me on edge. I kept waiting for Naomi to walk through the door like it was the most normal thing in the world, like nothing was out of the ordinary. There was something about her presence that made you feel like she owned every place she stepped into.

Was this some cruel joke, or was she really coming over? My heart raced, and for a second, I wondered if I was dreaming. Naomi showing up uninvited, at this hour? It didn't make sense. But then again, nothing about her ever did. I held my breath, hoping this would all blow over, but deep down, I knew I was bracing for the worst. She was the kind of surprise guest I couldn't say no to, and whenever she was around, everything seemed to get way more complicated. All I could do was wait and pray, hoping I wouldn't end up in the middle of another mess I didn't ask for.

It was almost comical, me peeking through the window like I was channeling my inner Malcolm X—minus the shotgun, of course. I had no idea what I was doing, but with Naomi threatening to show up at my door, it felt like my only option. My best move was to sit tight and hope she'd just give up and leave. She probably thought I'd been dodging her calls all day, so there was no point in texting or calling her back now.

I turned off all the lights in the apartment and shut down the TVs, like somehow Naomi couldn't spot the glow of the screen through the windows. I even double-checked that the curtains were tightly drawn, as if I was playing a high-stakes game of hide and seek with a ghost. I crawled into bed, pulling the covers up to my chin, and tried to convince myself this was just a bad dream—like maybe I'd wake up in a few hours and find out she'd never even gotten my address.

Then my phone buzzed loudly, making me jump so hard I almost launched myself out of bed. Not now, I thought, my heart racing. I grabbed the phone, half-expecting it to be Naomi, but was relieved to see a message from Will.

> Just sent you a Venmo. Don't spend it all at once. I'm planning to win that money back next week.

I smiled and checked Venmo. The $500 was there, just like Will promised. Feeling a bit better, I rolled over, thinking maybe Naomi's surprise visit was all in my head. But just as I started to relax, a loud knock at the door snapped me upright.

My heart went from zero to sixty. Could it really be her? I froze, clutching the covers like they were a life raft. The cold wood floor under me somehow made everything feel even more real, like I could feel every thud of my heart echoing through the apartment.

But no, it wasn't a dream. This was happening. My worst nightmare—my reality.

"James, open up," Naomi's voice cut through the quiet. "I know you're in there."

The knocking came again, louder and more urgent, like she was testing the door's ability to withstand a full assault. I could practically picture her on the other side, arms crossed, tapping her foot, waiting for me to make my move. Panic hit me like a tidal wave. I had two choices: answer the door and face Naomi head-on, or pretend I wasn't home and risk her calling in reinforcements—maybe the cops or, worse, a full-on search party.

I took a deep breath, bracing myself like I was about to face a firing squad, and opened the door. There she was, standing just on the other side, looking way too serious for this time of night. In one hand, she held a Bible; in the other, a spray bottle with a label that said "Holy Water."

"James, I'm here to cast out the demons from you and your house," Naomi said, holding up the bottle and aiming it directly at me.

"Uh, what demons?" I asked, glancing over my shoulder as if expecting to see something sinister lurking in the shadows

"The demons, James. The ones that come from skipping church and making bad choices. Now, let's have a little chat."

I glanced at the bottle again, then back at her. "So, are you here for an exorcism or just a really intense pep talk?" I asked, trying to keep it light as I stepped aside to let her in.

Naomi brushed past me, and I couldn't help but think, *What in the world is she doing here?*

# CHAPTER 23

*Facing many trials*

"COFFEE, TEA, OR… ME?" I JOKED, HOPING TO BREAK
the awkward silence and ignore the million questions running
through my head. Why was she really here?

She raised an eyebrow and gave me a little smirk. "Do you
have anything with a little more… kick?"

Before I could say a word, she breezed past me into the kitch-
en like she owned the place. Showing up uninvited was one thing,
but acting like she had a VIP pass? That was pushing it. I followed
her, half expecting her to start rearranging my furniture.

To my surprise, she went straight for my prized bottle of Dom
Perignon, then grabbed two champagne flutes and the opener. I
blinked. Holy water in one hand, Dom Perignon in the other?
Now things were getting strange.

Was she seriously about to pop open my most expensive bottle of champagne and use the matching fancy glasses? Wasn't she a pastor? I mean, isn't drinking supposed to be a sin or something? Sure, Jesus turned water into wine, but that was at a wedding, not in my kitchen just before midnight. I'd been saving that bottle for a special occasion, not for a surprise pop-in from an unexpected guest.

Something told me this night was about to get even *weirder*.

"This must've cost a pretty penny," she said, handing me the bottle and the opener like it was no big deal. "You don't mind, do you?" Before I could say anything, she was already heading back into the living room, with the flutes in one hand and my bag of Spicy Sweet Chili Doritos in the other. "I *love* these chips!"

*Why don't you just make yourself at home?* I thought, watching her crunch away on my Doritos. I was still fuming over the fact that I was about to open my best bottle of champagne for someone who'd just barged in.

And then, it hit me—I wasn't just mad at her. I was mad at her husband, too. What kind of guy lets his wife show up at a single guy's place this late?

First my champagne, now my Doritos… what would she take next, a kidney? Maybe she wasn't here to cast out demons. *Maybe she was here to steal my soul—or at least my snacks.*

"So, James," Naomi kicked off her shoes and sprawled out on the couch, giving me a look that seemed to say, *I'm all yours.* For a second, I found myself lost in a daydream of the two of us together. But reality snapped me back. What was I even thinking? I pushed the thought aside and poured her a glass of the pricey champagne.

"I bet you're wondering why I'm here, right?" she said, taking the glass from me with a sly smile.

"Yeah, you could say that," I replied, my voice barely louder than a whisper. I couldn't shake the feeling that life was playing some sort of prank on me. Here was someone beautiful and mysterious, right in my living room, and yet she felt totally unreachable. I took a long sip of my own champagne, hoping it would clear my head a bit. "So… what brings you here, Naomi?"

She took a deep breath, her gaze never leaving mine. "I need someone to talk to," she said softly, her voice carrying a hint of vulnerability. She stepped closer, her eyes locked on mine as if she was searching for something. "From the moment I saw you at church, I felt like we had a connection. Like I could really trust you."

She smiled, but her eyes held something deeper, like she was carrying a story she hadn't told anyone.

"Want to hear a secret, Naomi?" I said, leaning just enough to catch her attention.

She tilted her head, her eyes narrowing. "What secret?"

Her voice was soft but steady, and for a second, I thought about actually telling her. My jaw tightened, and I shifted back, shaking my head.

"Forget it," I muttered, forcing a smirk. "It's not that important."

Her lips pressed into a thin line, but she didn't argue. She just stood there, staring at me like she could pull the words out of my mouth if she tried hard enough.

"Someday," she said, her voice low but clear, "you're going to run out of things to hide."

I poured another glass, trying to steady my thoughts. How could I tell her the truth—that I had fallen for her? I knew it was wrong. She was married, and I'd buried these feelings long ago. But now, standing here with her so close, it was getting harder to keep my emotions in check.

"You look like you're off somewhere else," she said, watching me closely. "What's on your mind, James?"

I tried to act casual, shrugging it off. "It's nothing. I'm just... I don't know. Overthinking, I guess."

Naomi wasn't buying it. She leaned in a little, her eyes searching mine. "Are you sure? Because it feels like there's more to it."

I didn't know what to say. The truth was right there, on the tip of my tongue, but I couldn't let it out. She was too close. Her presence made it hard to think straight. Her hand brushed mine, and I felt a shock run through me.

"You know you can trust me, right?" Naomi's voice was soft, steady, but her eyes locked on mine like she was trying to read my mind. "If there's something you need to get off your chest…"

I shifted my stance, my gaze darting to the door, to the couch, to anywhere but her face.

"Well?" she pressed, leaning in, her presence crowding the room.

"Maybe…" My voice cracked. "Maybe you should go."

Her eyes stayed on mine, unmoving. Then, without a word, she slipped her hand into mine. Her fingers were warm, firm, and somehow more convincing than her voice.

"Is that really what you want?"

I stared at her, the words caught somewhere between my chest and throat. She didn't flinch—just stood there, waiting.

But what could I say?

The silence grew, but I still couldn't bring myself to break it. Not yet.

# CHAPTER 24

## Create in me a pure heart

WHAT ABOUT GOD? WHAT ABOUT HER HUSBAND? SHE had to know this was wrong—every part of it. My mind raced as we stood there, barely inches apart. I couldn't shake the thought that she was supposed to be the one people looked up to, someone strong and spiritual, not... here with me.

I thought of that tree in the Garden of Eden—the one that looked so good but came with a price. This felt exactly like that. It was tempting, but the consequences hung heavy in the air. Her hand brushed mine, and my heart pounded so hard it drowned out everything else.

I wanted to step back, say something, do something to stop this. But I couldn't. We were too close now, the space between us shrinking, our breaths meeting in the stillness. My mind screamed, **don't do it,** but every other part of me pulled toward her.

We were right there, on the edge, ready to cross a line I knew we couldn't uncross.

Her beautiful brown eyes sparkled, and for the first time, I saw my soul resting there, calm, as if it had been waiting all along. The moment hit before I could brace for it. Suddenly, I grabbed her by the waist, pulling her close. The faint scent of vanilla and strawberries filled the air as I held her, and it nearly unraveled me. "I want you... more than you know," I whispered, the words slipping out faster than I could think. The room seemed to hold its breath, suspended between what we knew was right and the undeniable pull of what was happening. Her eyes locked with mine, and for a heartbeat, the world vanished. That line I swore I'd never cross was right there, but now it was blurred, almost gone, as everything else faded into the space between us.

She closed her eyes and leaned her head against my chest, like she belonged there. My heart was going crazy—pounding so loud I was sure she could hear it. What was I doing? Every alarm in my brain screamed stop, but my arms stayed locked around her. A married woman. I should've felt guilty, ashamed, some-thing... but instead, it just felt right. And that terrified me.

"You okay?" I asked, kissing her gently on the forehead. It felt like something from a movie, but this wasn't a scene. This was real—and it made everything feel even more complicated.

"I'm where I belong," she whispered. Then came the words I wasn't ready for. "I've fallen for you, James."

"I feel the same way," I said before I could stop myself. The pull to kiss her grew stronger, but as I leaned in, an image hit me—Eve, biting the forbidden fruit and handing it to Adam. That moment of knowing it was wrong but doing it anyway.

The thought hit me hard. I let go and stepped back, like snapping out of a dream. "We can't do this," I said. It felt like we were teetering on the edge of something dangerous, knowing one wrong step would send us over.

Suddenly, her phone rang, shattering the tension between us like glass. She glanced at the screen, her face tightening. I already knew. It was her husband.

"Give me a minute," she uttered softly, turning on her heel and walking into the kitchen.

I sank back, staring at the bottle of Dom Perignon on the table, the reality of what was happening crashing over me. What had I been thinking? Imagining we could ever have something real—it was crazy. The enemy was playing with me, tempting me into believing something impossible. I grabbed the bottle and took a long swig, letting the bitterness of the champagne settle in my chest. Fool, I thought to myself, staring at the empty space where she'd just stood.

Minutes passed before Naomi reappeared, her face drained, as if she'd seen something that left its mark on her—something she couldn't shake off.

"I have to go," she said, snatching up her purse, keys, and that ever-present bottle of holy water—like it might shield her from what had just happened.

"Is everything alright?" I asked, though we both knew the answer. She was being pulled back to the life she had, the life she was supposed to live.

She hesitated, eyes locked on mine like she wanted to say more but couldn't. Then she stepped in, arms around my neck, and kissed my cheek. "I'm sorry."

I didn't move. Not when she turned, not when she walked out. The door clicked shut, and everything that followed felt like it never happened.

# CHAPTER 25



FOR THE NEXT FEW MONTHS, I KEPT MY DISTANCE FROM anything that felt like church and from married women. Not that I was looking to get tangled up with one—just my luck that the only woman who made me feel alive was already off-limits.

It was just after 5:00 p.m. on Friday when I walked into Gold's Gym, ready for a workout I desperately needed. The place was alive with energy, and people focused on their own routines, but I had one thing on my mind—trying to shake the thoughts of Naomi. I knew the gym would help, even if just for a little while.

With my Spotify playlist pounding in my ears, I focused on the weight bench, shutting out the noise in my head. I loaded 225 pounds onto the bar and lay back, my grip firm on the steel. This wasn't just a workout—it was a prayer, each lift an offering, each rep a plea for strength to carry more than just the weight in front of me.

Just as I was about to dive into my set, my phone buzzed in my pocket. It was Will. He never called during workouts—he knew I liked to focus on my gains, not on gossip. I figured this must be important.

"What's up, Will?" I grunted, adjusting the weights and preparing for the first lift. "You know my workout schedule better than anyone, so this better be good."

"Listen, playboy," he said with a laugh. "So what if that married woman broke your heart? It's not the end of the world."

Thank God for my Dre Beats. Without them, those two cute women a few feet away would've probably started laughing too. "No one broke my heart," I said, forcing a grin I didn't feel. "I haven't even seen her in months. Probably for the best, anyway."

"True that, true that," he replied. "But isn't Virginia the state for lovers?"

"Yeah, so what of it?" I said, starting my first set of ten. The bar moved easily—too easy to be a distraction.

"Seriously? Out of all the single women in the 'lover's state,' you go for a married one? And a pastor?"

My jaw tightened at the thought. Ridiculous. I was trying to get my life together, not complicate it further.

He was really starting to get under my skin. I racked another fifty pounds on the bar and knocked out ten more reps, surprisingly smooth. Maybe it was adrenaline, maybe just pure stubbornness, but I felt unstoppable. Still, this conversation wasn't heading anywhere good. "Did you actually have something important to say, or is this it?"

"The truth shall set you free!" he laughed.

"Okay, I've got to go," I said, irritation creeping into my voice. I quickly stripped off the two twenty-five-pound plates and replaced them with a couple of forty-fives. 315 pounds. No sweat.

A small crowd gathered nearby, watching. Perfect. Nothing like a little pressure to sharpen the mind. I settled under the bar, my hands gripping the steel. "Lord, don't let me fail here," I whispered, eyes fixed.

"You still there?" Will asked, clueless that all eyes were on me, and I was about to put everything on the line.

"Yeah, give me a minute," I said, gripping the bar like it held the answer to everything. Deep breath. Focus. One rep, two, three—each one smoother than the last. By the eighth, the bar practically flew up, and for a moment, I felt unstoppable.

I added another twenty-five pounds to each side—365 pounds now. This wasn't just about the workout anymore. It was about proving something, even if I wasn't sure what or to who.

"Be with me, Lord," I said, hands gripping the bar. I locked my eyes on the weight, blocking everything else out. "One, two, three, four…" Each rep felt like breaking free, and by five, I had done it.

I checked my phone. Will had hung up, but a text message from him lit up the screen. I hadn't read it yet, but the anticipation was enough to lift my spirits after everything. It was the kind of boost I needed, after the weight I'd just lifted—both in the gym and in my mind.

Sorry for hanging up, man. My wife walked in, making sure I was getting ready for church.

I know you've been going through it with Naomi—at least, I think that's her name. LOL. Just messing with you.

But hey, I wanted to surprise you. I got two courtside tickets for the Celtics vs. Lakers game this Monday. Pack your bags and book a flight; get here by Sunday.

While we're on the sidelines cheering for the Celtics, we can talk smack to LeBron and that losing franchise, have some beers and good food, and watch our boys take the win.

And seriously, don't beat yourself up. God's got big plans for you. Whether or not that involves anyone from the church, let Him guide you. You know what happens when you take control—total disaster. LOL.

Hit me back. Peace, JB.

Two hours later, after staring at my phone and rereading Will's text more times than I'd care to admit, I finally gave in and booked my flight. Boston, here I come. Maybe a change of scenery was exactly what I needed.

# CHAPTER 26

Forgetting what is behind

WALKING INTO THE TD GARDEN FELT SURREAL, LIKE stepping into a dream I didn't know I had. The excitement in the arena rushed through me before I even found my seat. Center court, floor level—just a few feet away from LeBron James, Jason Tatum, and Jaylen Brown. I could practically feel their energy, and yeah, even their sweat. They were that close.

Everywhere I looked, history stared back at me. Championship banners hung proudly in the rafters, legends etched into the fabric of the building. It was electric. My heart was racing like a kid about to meet his heroes for the first time.

Then there were the fans—die-hards decked out in green, chanting like their lives depended on it. Gorgeous women wandered around, some flashing me smiles, others slipping me their numbers as they passed. Maybe they thought I was someone important, sitting in seats that cost more than a mortgage payment.

I couldn't stop grinning. This was more than a game. This was a moment I'd be telling people about for the rest of my life.

"What did you have to do to score these tickets? And on Martin Luther King Day, no less?" I asked Will, raising an eyebrow. He shot me a grin, the kind that told me I probably didn't want to know the answer.

"Some secrets are better left untold," he said, chuckling. "But since we're boys, I can show you better than I can tell you."

Before I could respond, Will got up and made his way down toward the Celtics bench, weaving through the crowd like he owned the place. He stopped to chat with a tall, sharply dressed guy who looked like he was part of the coaching staff. They were laughing and talking like old friends. I sat there, trying to figure out what kind of strings Will had pulled. I hadn't seen him have a drink yet, so this wasn't just him being his usual wild self. But then again, this was Will—Mr. Unpredictable.

A few moments later, Will turned and pointed in my direction. My first instinct was to look behind me, thinking he was gesturing at someone else. Nope. It was me.

The two of them headed my way, laughing like they shared some secret. I wasn't sure whether to stand my ground or prepare for whatever was coming.

"So, this is the guy with a thing for married women?" he said, smirking like he already knew the whole story.

They both erupted in laughter, leaving me frozen in my seat, unsure whether to laugh along or crawl under the floor.

I shot Will a look sharp enough to make him flinch. What was he thinking, running his mouth like that? Loyalty clearly wasn't his strong suit. Sure, only a few people were close enough to hear him, but it felt like the whole arena—all 17,000 seats— had turned their attention to me. My stomach knotted, the guilt creeping in, even though I hadn't done anything… yet.

I forced a tight smile, swallowing my pride. Will, oblivious to the death stare I was giving him, introduced me to his buddy like everything was cool. The two of them kept laughing, clearly enjoying the joke—me.

Will, always the comedian, dropped to one knee, throwing his hands up like some preacher delivering a sermon. "In the name of Jesus, stay away from my wife!" he declared, his voice loud enough to draw a few amused glances from nearby.

They doubled over, laughing like it was the funniest thing they'd ever seen, practically holding each other up. Just my luck, a couple of players on the court glanced over, probably trying to figure out what the fuss was about. My face burned as I dropped into my seat, arms crossed tight like a kid in trouble.

"We're just messing with you," Will said, playfully jabbing me in the chest. Then, with a grin that didn't quite reach his eyes, he added, "But seriously, stay away from married women."

I sighed, sinking into my seat. Great—just what I needed. An audience and a lecture.

A few minutes before the game kicked off, I spotted some familiar faces in the crowd—celebrities, rappers, and coaches—all waving at me like I was part of their elite circle. I couldn't help but grin and wave back, soaking in the attention. For one night, I felt like I belonged to that millionaire club, whatever that meant.

By the end of the third quarter, the Celtics were crushing the Lakers, and I was loving every second. The energy in the arena felt alive, and I found myself yelling along with the crowd. For once, Naomi wasn't on my mind—until the woman next to me laughed. It was the same laugh Naomi had, sharp and quick, like she was trying not to let it out but couldn't help herself. Suddenly, she was all I could think about. Still, the Celtics were winning, so for a little while, life was almost perfect.

Instead of crashing in Boston, I grabbed a red-eye back to Virginia. Boston might have been where I was born, but Virginia felt like home now, and I was itching to get back to familiar ground. The adrenaline from the game still pulsed through me, and for once, I felt lighter—like I was actually ready to face whatever came next.

I slept through the flight, waking up just in time to shuffle off the plane like a zombie. By the time I got home, all I wanted was to crash. That plan lasted about five seconds—until I spotted the pink envelope on the floor.

At first, I thought maybe it was junk mail. You know, the kind that promises a free cruise or some other scam. But no, this was different. Too deliberate. Too... pink.

I picked it up, holding it like it might explode. No name. No address. Just a pastel mystery waiting to ruin my night.

Back in bed, I turned it over in my hands, stalling. Part of me thought, *Maybe it's not that serious. Maybe it's just a Hallmark card.* The other part was screaming, *Don't open it!* I ignored both and tore it open anyway.

That's when the scent hit— vanilla and strawberries. Naomi. Of course, it was her. She had a way of showing up even when she wasn't actually there, like some kind of psycho ex-girlfriend.

I unfolded the paper, my hands shaking just enough to annoy me. The words on the page hit hard, knocking every last ounce of peace I had left right out the window.

# CHAPTER 27

## These three remain: Faith, Hope and Love

NAOMI'S LETTER BEGAN WITH **LOVE NEVER FAILS** written in bold at the top, like it belonged in a greeting card—or maybe a sermon. Beneath it, the rest of the message was written in the neatest handwriting I'd ever seen—on a blank sheet of paper. Impressive.

My Dearest Brother James,

It's been months since I last saw you, and every moment apart has been its own kind of torture. Walking out of your apartment that day was one of the hardest decisions I've ever had to make. Please believe me when I say it wasn't about you—it was about me. You are an extraordinary person, and I thank God every day that our paths crossed.

I felt my chest tighten, not sure if I was ready for what came next.

I need to tell you something—something I thought I'd take to the grave... until I met you. The first night you walked into church, I wasn't surprised. I knew you'd be there. How? Divine intervention. I'd been praying for you, James, for three years. I asked God for signs, miracles, and wonders—and somehow, you turned out to be all three. Let me explain...

Her words gripped me, and I could feel the weight of what was coming, bracing myself for the explanation that might change everything.

When I called you out and spoke a prophecy over you, that was real. No gimmicks, no tricks—just a word from God. And when I asked you to run around the church three times, I saw the hesitation in your eyes. You thought it was a joke, didn't you? But then you went for it—boots flopping, pants sagging, running like your life depended on it. To everyone else, you might've looked a little ridiculous. But that's not what I saw. I saw your obedience.

I paused, letting out a small laugh as I thought about that run—people staring, some whispering. At the time, it didn't seem like much, just something I did. But Naomi had seen it differently.

When I laid my hands on you and you fell... I knew it wasn't real. You weren't having some "Holy Ghost experience" like everyone thought. But I understood why you did it. You weren't trying to deceive anyone—you were trying to protect me from embarrassment. And for that, I'm sorry. I never should've put you in that position.

I stopped reading for a moment, letting her words sink in. She was right. I hadn't been swept up in the moment—I was just trying to save her from looking bad in front of all those people. Shaking my head, I got up, grabbed a cold beer from the fridge, and dropped onto the couch, letter still in hand.

Do I believe in the Holy Spirit? Absolutely. But I never expected you to fall like the others. Maybe I was the only one—aside from God—who knew you wouldn't. But here's the thing: I believe in divine signs, and that night was one of them. Sometimes, what happens isn't meant for everyone to see, only for those who are meant to understand.

I took a sip from the bottle, her words turning over in my mind. That night wasn't just a church service—it was something deeper. Something I still couldn't fully understand.

When you walked out of the church that night, I didn't think I'd ever see you again. You were just a first-time visitor—why would you come back? But that night, I couldn't get you out of my mind. I prayed and asked God for a sign, hoping somehow our paths would cross again. Then, the very next day, there you were, standing in line at Dunkin' Donuts. My heart jumped. Right then and there, I thanked God for answering my prayer. It felt like a sign, and for a moment, I truly believed dreams could come true.

I smiled to myself, thinking back to that random encounter at Dunkin' Donuts. At the time, it felt like pure coincidence—but Naomi was weaving it into something far bigger, something I hadn't considered.

I know what you're probably thinking—who believes in dreams, right? Well, I do. Especially prophetic ones. When I saw you in that line, I felt ready to pour my heart out to a stranger. There was something about you, something different. And when you touched me—when I was at my most vulnerable—it sparked something in me I'll never forget.

Heat rushed to my chest. My palms were sweaty, and my heart was pounding like it was ready to burst out of my chest. "This is deep," I whispered to myself, grabbing the beer for a quick sip to steady my nerves. I let out a long breath, then dove back into the letter, bracing myself for whatever came next.

I paused, staring at Naomi's words, feeling their weight. This wasn't just a letter—it felt like a confession, a revelation, a glimpse into a part of her heart she'd kept hidden.

*Inside Dunkin' Donuts, when our eyes met, I saw something deeper. I saw my soul in yours. But it was the third time we crossed paths that sealed it for me. What were the odds, James? You and I speaking at the same event, on the same stage, in a state neither of us called home? Some might call it coincidence, but I call it divine destiny.*

My heart raced as I read that. *Divine destiny?* It all seemed impossible, yet something about it felt too real to ignore.

*James, you are everything I have ever wanted, prayed for, and hoped to find in a man.*

I sank back into the couch, swallowing hard as my throat went dry. She had prayed for me? For me? I wasn't sure how to process that.

*There's one last thing I need to tell you before I finish this letter. The night you showed up at church, I prayed for you* specifically. I asked God for a sign, but I was a little sneaky about it. I wanted to see if He'd answer my prayer with the details I was hoping for.

I felt the tension building as I braced myself for what was coming next. This wasn't just a random encounter—it felt planned, intentional. I could barely sit still, the anticipation rising as I held her letter, like it was the key to a mystery I hadn't even realized I was part of.

I asked God to send a man to the church wearing a green shirt, blue jeans, and boots. You might think that's just a coincidence, but I was incredibly specific in my prayers. I prayed for a strong, handsome man, wearing a striped green shirt that caught the light just right, Levi jeans that fit perfectly, and Timberland boots that seemed to echo with purpose. And then, like a miracle, there you were—standing right in front of me, exactly as I had imagined.

I know this probably sounds crazy, and I'm sure you're sitting on your favorite couch with a cold beer nearby, wondering why I'm reaching out now.

My chest tightened as I read those words again. *How did she know?*

Naomi had prayed for a man in a green striped shirt, Levi's jeans, and Timberland boots. It wasn't just the clothes—it was the timing, the church, everything. She had been so specific, and somehow, there I was—unknowingly checking every box in her prayer. But what really threw me was her knowing I'd be sitting on my couch with a beer.

I stood up from the couch, still holding the letter, and looked around the room like Naomi might suddenly appear from behind a curtain. The blinds were shut, the door was locked, and everything was quiet. But I couldn't shake the feeling she was watching me.

I walked to the window, pulled the blinds aside, and glanced outside. The street was empty. No sign of anyone.

"Okay, I'm officially losing it," I muttered, trying to calm myself down. I checked every room in the apartment—closets, under the bed, even behind the shower curtain—just to make sure. No one. *It had to be the exhaustion*, or maybe the leftover adrenaline from the game. Yeah, that's probably it.

Still a little shaken, I dropped back onto the couch, grabbed the letter from the table, and took another sip of my beer, trying to calm myself and see what else Naomi had to say.

There's something about you, James. Something in your eyes speaks to my soul, like a song I didn't know I was waiting for. That night in your apartment, when my head rested on your chest, I heard your heart—it felt like it was calling my name. It was a rhythm that felt like home. For the first time in years, I felt safe. All my fears and doubts seemed to disappear. I'd never felt so seen, so understood.

Maybe I've said too much, but here's the truth: whenever you think of me, remember that I love you. Only you. I felt it the moment you looked at me—a connection so deep it scared me.

Naomi.

P.S. You already have the answers to the questions you're asking about me. Look within, then pray. God has revealed you to me; now He needs to reveal me to you. Sleep well, Man of God.

What was this? I sank back into the couch, staring at the letter in my hands. Excited and scared didn't even begin to cover it. Could this really be happening? Naomi had poured her heart out, and deep down, I couldn't lie to myself—I loved her too. This felt bigger than a crush; it felt... real.

But then it hit me—she was married. Why would she tell me she loved me when she belonged to someone else? How could this possibly be right?

I started pacing the room, trying to make sense of it all. Why hadn't she mentioned her husband? And why would she pull me into this? It wasn't right—not to me, not to him. And what about God? How could this possibly be acceptable to Him? Love wasn't supposed to come wrapped in lies and complications. No matter how much I cared for her, I couldn't ignore the fact that this was wrong. She had opened a door, but it wasn't one I could step through—not without losing a part of myself and everything I believed in.

I felt stuck between two worlds—one promising love and the other bound by rules I couldn't ignore. How could I want her so much, knowing how tangled this all was? I'd never felt this way about anyone, and the idea of letting her go made my chest tighten, even though she was never mine to begin with.

I walked to my bedroom, the letter in one hand and the half-empty beer in the other, unsure what to do with her confession—or the guilt that clung to me like a shadow.

Lying on the bed, I stared at the ceiling fan, my thoughts tugging me in opposite directions. It felt like I was on both sides of the rope, pulling against myself. Deep down, though, I couldn't shake the feeling that there was something real between us.

"What if Naomi's trapped in a dead-end marriage? What if I'm her way out?" I mumbled.

But then the harder questions hit. Was it worth it? Could I really pursue a love built on someone else's vows?

I slid out of bed and made my way to the bathroom, trying to clear my head. You need to figure this out. Is it love, or just a dangerous distraction? One wrong move could change everything.

Maybe, just maybe, it wasn't Naomi who was the crazy one—it was me.

# CHAPTER 28

## *Stop doubting and believe*

IT WAS 7:30 P.M. ON A FRIDAY WHEN I CASUALLY WALKED into *House of Blessings Christian Center*, a small but growing church in the heart of Richmond, Virginia. Originally, I was supposed to be speaking at a conference in New York, but a snowstorm shut everything down. The event was canceled, yet they still paid me in full, so I wasn't complaining. With nowhere else to be, I figured, why not stop by?

To be honest, I'd been avoiding churches for a while. I told myself I was done with them, tired of the noise and judgment. But tonight, with everything going on in my life—like being in love with a married woman and convincing myself that it wasn't entirely wrong—maybe this was exactly where I needed to be. Better here than lost in my own thoughts.

When I stepped inside the sanctuary, I noticed a group of about twenty older men, casually dressed, sitting together on the right side of the church, chatting among themselves. I didn't feel like joining in, so I found a seat toward the back, hoping to stay unnoticed. As I passed by, one of the men, a tall, bald guy wearing a number 56 New York Giants jersey, gave me a nod and waved me over.

"Come on up front with us, brother," he said.

"Thanks, but I'm good right here," I replied, giving a polite smile. I wasn't in the mood to socialize, even if it might have come off as a little standoffish. The last time I sat in the front row at a church, I got called out by Naomi claiming to have a message from God just for me. That wasn't an experience I needed to relive.

To avoid sitting there like some kid in time-out, I lowered my head and pretended to pray, my lips moving just enough to sell it. I had become pretty skilled at blending in during these moments. When I opened my eyes, a muscular, light-skinned guy walked in, wearing a sleeveless shirt under a black leather motorcycle vest. The words "Fear None but God" were printed boldly across the back, and he carried a black motorcycle helmet at his side.

He gave me a once-over, like he was sizing me up, then raised two fingers in the air. "What's up, MOG?" he said in a deep voice.

I nodded back, playing it cool, though inwardly, I was judging him for strolling into church looking like he had just walked off a biker rally. Who wears that in church? But before I could ride that thought too far, guilt hit me like a brick. The memory of Naomi flashed across my mind—me and her, tangled in something we shouldn't be. Who was I to judge anyone?

He walked down the aisle, greeting the older men like he was a regular, all smiles and handshakes. Meanwhile, I was hiding out in the back, trying to go unnoticed. A few minutes later, though, he was back, standing near my row with a serious look on his face.

"Mind if I sit here?" His voice caught me off guard—softer than I'd expected, more Mike Tyson than the Barry White act he'd pulled earlier. I stood to let him slide into the row, and he flashed a quick smile before plopping his helmet onto the seat between us.

He reached out his hand. "My name's Bryce, but my friends— *only* my friends—call me Big B."

"I'm James," I replied, trying to sound tough as I shook his hand. "But *everyone* calls me JB."

"Nice to meet you, *James*," he said, completely ignoring the nickname I'd just offered. He took his seat, stretching out like he owned the place, and I could already tell this was going to be a long night.

What I didn't expect was for him to start talking to me like I was his personal therapist. He jumped right in, rattling off details about his life without skipping a beat. At first, I tuned him out—I wasn't here to bond with a stranger; I had enough on my plate. But there was something about the way he talked, like he needed to get it all out, that made me listen.

Turns out Bryce—Big B.—wasn't just some random biker. He was a federal agent moonlighting as a bounty hunter. And here I was, pegging him as some outlaw, acting like I had him all figured out.

Funny how people surprise you.

I kept my conversation with Bryce short. I didn't know him, and I wasn't about to start spilling my life story to a guy who walked into church looking like he'd just come from a biker bar. Trust didn't come easy for me, especially not with someone who gave off drifter vibes.

At exactly 8 o'clock, a guy who could've been Terrell Owens' long-lost twin swaggered onto the stage. His blue-and-white Nike sweatsuit practically glowed under the lights, and he carried himself like he was about to deliver the halftime speech of the century.

He snatched the mic off the podium, gave it a few confident taps, and grinned like he knew every eye in the room was locked on him.

"Welcome, mighty men of God!" he boomed, his voice bouncing off the walls. "Tonight is going to be a life-changing experience for all of us."

Meanwhile, Bryce was in his own world, hunched over his phone, thumbs moving at warp speed. He was probably texting someone far more interesting than a room full of men.

I leaned over, cupped my hands, and half-yelled, "Amen!"

That got him. He jumped, nearly flinging his phone. "Amen," he laughed, giving me a side-eye. "Good one, James. Or should I say, JB?"

On stage, the speaker kept rolling. "Tonight, it's just us men. No women. No distractions. This is our Men's Trip Conference, and fellas, we're the stars of this movie."

"Praise the Lord!" someone shouted from the front row like they'd been waiting all day to say it.

"It's about time!" another voice called out, drawing a wave of laughter.

"And for those of you who are married—which is probably most of us in the room," the speaker said, pointing to the crowd, "go ahead and loosen that belt. Stop sucking in your gut and let it hang over those pants! Your wife isn't here to judge you."

The room exploded with laughter. Even I had to laugh, shaking my head.

For a split second, it worked. Thoughts of Naomi and her being married eased to the back of my mind, quiet but not gone. Heavy things like that don't vanish with a joke—they just step aside for a moment.

I looked around the room. Wedding rings were everywhere, a small detail I hadn't noticed before. Even Bryce had one, a plain black band resting on his hand like it had always been there. I swallowed hard. Was this some kind of married men's support group?

Then the thought hit me: what if Naomi's husband was here? Sitting somewhere in this very room? What were the chances? Same room, same night—it couldn't be, right?

I shifted in my seat, reaching for my truck keys buried in my pocket. The exit door caught my eye. I mapped out the route in my head: aisle, door, parking lot, freedom.

"You good?" Bryce asked, his tone serious. "You look like you just seen a ghost, or spotted the husband of the woman you've been entangled with."

He laughed, slapping me hard on the back.

Wait, what? My stomach dropped at his sudden comment. His stare pinned me, sharp enough that for a split second, I thought about standing up and confessing to the whole room: Yeah, I'm attracted to a married woman, and maybe she's married to one of you. The guilt had to be written all over my face.

But instead of spilling my secret to a room full of strangers, I wiped the sweat off my forehead with the back of my hand and forced a shaky smile.

"Nah, nothing like that," I said, though the crack in my voice wasn't doing me any favors. "It's just… when he mentioned married men, I thought maybe I stumbled into the wrong conference."

Bryce let out a loud laugh, catching the attention of a few men seated up front. He gave me a light pat on the shoulder and leaned in close. "This conference is for all men, not just the married ones."

I slipped my keys back into my pocket, relieved my secret was safe. "Good to know."

But Bryce wasn't done. He rubbed his chin, studying me like he was solving a riddle. "You're not messing around with one of these married guys' wives, are you?" He asked, his gave following mine like he was a detective following a lead.

"Who, me?" I nearly choked on my own words. "No! Are you crazy? I'm not a homewrecker. I'm just here to hear from God, like everyone else." I paused, fumbling for something to steady the moment. "I've just… been going through a lot lately. Only God can get me through it."

Bryce's face softened, his tone calm. "You're in the right place, then. This is one of the best churches in Virginia. The word of God is spoken unapologetically here. No games, no gimmicks. Just the truth. So, whatever you're dealing with? Hand it over to Him."

His words hit harder than I expected. Maybe it was the way he said it, or maybe I was just tired of running from the truth, but for the first time in a while, I felt like I was exactly where I needed to be.

"Much respect," I muttered, not sure what else to say. Bryce was right. God could see me through whatever I was going through. At least, that's what I kept telling myself. But deep down, I wasn't fully convinced. Faith was something I talked about more than I actually lived.

For the next hour, the room filled with stories. Men from all walks of life, sharing their struggles, victories, and pain. It was raw. Real. Each testimony made me feel more vulnerable, chipping away at the walls I'd put up. At one point, I even considered sharing my own battle, but fear got the best of me. What if they didn't understand? What if I said too much?

I looked around the room—men of different races and backgrounds, all wrestling with their own demons, yet here they were, standing firm in their faith. Even though I stayed silent, I felt a strange sense of belonging. Maybe, just maybe, I was in the right place after all.

At around 9:00 p.m., the guy in the Nike suit returned to the stage, smiling as he grabbed the mic again. "Tonight has been an amazing night, and I'm proud of all of you," he said. "Before we wrap things up, I'd like to sing a song that's dear to my heart. It's called 'O Come to the Altar' by Elevation Worship."

As the music flowed through the church speakers, I closed my eyes, letting it wash over me. The rhythm, slow and steady, found its way to my core. I tapped my foot in time, feeling something stir deep within. It wasn't just the melody—it was the way the song seemed to speak directly to the part of me I'd kept hidden for so long.

Then he started to sing.

His voice was so pure, so full of emotion, it caught me off guard. For the first time that night, I felt like God was talking to me, as if He was using that man's voice to reach me. The words, "come to the altar," echoed in my mind, playing over and over, sinking into my soul. I couldn't hold back any longer. My chest tightened, and without warning, the tears started falling.

It was as if Jesus Himself was whispering to me, telling me to let it go. Telling me that everything was going to be okay. All the doubts, the guilt, the confusion swirling inside me—it didn't stand a chance against the peace that was slowly taking over. *Trust Me,* I heard. *Give Me all your problems... even Naomi.* Maybe that's what she meant when she said to look inside.

I bowed my head and prayed, really prayed. For the first time in what felt like forever, I asked God for guidance, for clarity. I surrendered, letting go of the weight I'd been carrying, while the words of that song—the most beautiful words I'd ever heard—wrapped around me like a blanket.

When the music finally faded, I wiped my face quickly, hoping no one saw the mess I'd become.

When the final prayer ended, I stood, picked up my Bible, and exchanged handshakes with a few of the men. Their easy smiles carried a sense of camaraderie I hadn't anticipated. Just as I headed toward the exit, a firm hand landed on my shoulder. I turned to see Bryce.

"We should exchange numbers," he said, already pulling out his phone. "Are you cool with that?"

I just stood there, momentarily lost in thought, staring off into space. Something had shifted inside me tonight, something profound. I couldn't shake the feeling that I wouldn't be the same after this experience. Was this my own Damascus Road moment, like Paul had? A turning point that could change everything?

I snapped back to reality, looking at Bryce and nodding. "Yeah, I'm cool with it." I reached for my phone, feeling a mixture of gratitude and uncertainty about what lay ahead.

"Are you OK?" Bryce asked, concern etched on his face.

"Got a lot on my mind," I admitted, calling out my number as he entered it into his phone. He gave me a reassuring pat on the shoulder, then tapped it again.

"I'll give you a call this week. But I'll send you a text in a few to make sure you know it's me. It was good meeting you, brother JB. Have a good night and get home safely."

"You, too." I said, forcing a smile.

He hopped on his motorcycle, strapped on his helmet and glasses, then revved the engine a few times before shooting out of the parking lot, leaving me alone with my thoughts.

It turned out to be a great night after all. I met some cool guys, and for the first time in a while, I felt a real connection with God. After offering a few halfhearted goodbye, I climbed into my truck and drove home.

The second I stepped through my apartment door, my phone buzzed. A message from an unfamiliar number lit up the screen, making me freeze in place:

It's Bryce Adams from church tonight. Hope you got home safe. I'll give you a call tomorrow. Peace!

Wait, what? It couldn't be. No way. Bryce and Naomi couldn't possibly share the same last name… could they? My stomach dropped. What did this mean? Was Bryce… Naomi's husband?

# CHAPTER 29

*Let the Spirit change the way you think*

ON SUNDAY MORNING, I STARED OUT THE BEDROOM window as the sunrise painted the sky in streaks of orange and pink, casting a soft glow over everything. It felt like one of those mornings full of promise, where anything seemed possible. Determined to finally uncover the truth about Bryce and Naomi, I decided to play detective.

But my search hit a dead end. I scoured the internet for anything—a clue, a connection, anything at all. Nothing. No social media accounts, no LinkedIn, no Facebook, no Instagram. Even Google came up empty. Desperate, I tried searching for a church website, hoping for a members' directory or a photo gallery. Nothing there either.

What kind of church didn't have a website?

That realization hit me hard: I was stalking them. This wasn't who I was. Was my mind playing tricks on me? Was I trapped in a surreal dream, or had I become uncomfortably fixated on Naomi?

Dressed in all black, I felt like a shadow of the Black Panther—powerful, yet missing the mask. I snatched my keys from the basket in the hallway and stepped outside, ready to hunt down the missing pieces of my puzzle.

Ten minutes later, I merged onto Interstate 76, gripping the wheel tighter than usual. Meek Mill's "Going Bad" with Drake played through the speakers, but I barely heard it. My mind was racing as fast as the truck, weaving through traffic like I had somewhere important to be—which, for once, I did.

When I reached the exit, I eased off the gas, letting the truck slow to a normal speed. The closer I got to the church, the heavier everything felt. My chest tightened, and for a second, I wondered if I was ready for what I might find.

The church parking lot looked more like a luxury car show than a place of worship. I pulled into an open spot in the back, sliding in next to a green four-door Porsche and a candy apple red Corvette Stingray. If nothing else, one thing was obvious—there was serious money parked outside the house of God today.

After a quick prayer and popping a peppermint Altoid, I grabbed my Bible from the passenger seat and headed for the entrance. Each step felt deliberate, like I was walking into a board-room about to seal a high-stakes deal. A part of me even imagined theme music playing in the background, setting the tone for whatever I might uncover inside. If nothing else, I figured, I'd walk away with a story worth sharing Monday morning.

Climbing the stairs to the entrance, I was met by the warm smiles of two well-dressed Black women standing by the double doors. Their presence radiated a sense of comfort that instantly made the church feel inviting.

"Welcome home," one of them said, handing me a program along with a small white envelope boldly labeled **MY OFFERING**.

"Thank you," I replied, matching her energy. I slipped the envelope discreetly into my Bible like it held some kind of secret message.

One of the women gestured toward the sanctuary doors. As I walked in, I opened the program booklet. It detailed the *Ten-Year Pastor's Anniversary Service*, featuring a lineup of guest pastors from churches all over the country—a roll call of spiritual heavyweights. But one thing stopped me in my tracks. Naomi's name wasn't listed anywhere. Instead, under the church leadership, there was Pastor Daniel Rinaldi, founder of *Standing on God's Truth Ministry*.

The plot thickens, I thought, as the inner sanctuary doors

swung open and I stepped inside, curiosity swirling in my mind. What was really going on here?

"Follow me," said a green-eyed woman with a sprinkle of freckles across her nose, her fitted blue and green dress accentuating her athletic frame as she moved with purpose. As she led me down the aisle, the scent of polished wood and fresh flowers filled the air, mingling with the hum of voices from the congregation. She glanced back over her shoulder, one eyebrow arched like she was silently asking, *You good back there?*

"Is everything okay?" I asked, my eyes scanning the sea of faces, searching for Naomi and Bryce among the vibrant dresses and sharp suits.

Her playful grin broke out before I even had a chance to finish. "Wait, I remember you!" she said, a teasing light in her eyes as we approached an empty row. "You're the guy who was running around the church in those big boots, right? The one who looked like he was about to lose his pants any second?"

A laugh escaped before I could stop it. "Yeah, that was me," I admitted, rubbing the back of my neck.

She burst out laughing, loud enough to draw a few curious glances from nearby rows. "I swear, I thought you were gonna wipe out at least three deacons before you made it back to your seat!"

I smirked. "Well, you know what they say—go big or go home."

"Oh, you definitely went big. And don't think I didn't notice your Timberlands flopping halfway off your feet. I thought they'd come flying off and take somebody out!" Her freckles seemed to dance as she laughed, her energy contagious.

"Glad I could make a lasting impression," I said, shaking my head but unable to keep from grinning.

She tilted her head, still smiling. "Don't worry, though—I thought it was kind of cute. Maybe we can hang out sometime, you know?"

"Are you asking me out in the middle of church?" I shot back, the corners of my mouth twitching upward.

"Maybe I am," she said with a shrug. "Enjoy the service, *Timberland Track Star*." With a playful turn, she headed back toward the lobby, leaving me wondering if I'd just walked into something unexpected.

For a brief moment, I forgot about Naomi entirely. That green-eyed woman had a way of stealing the spotlight.

As the service began, the choir took the stage, their voices rising in worship. But I barely noticed. My mind kept circling back to the freckled woman and what she'd said before she walked away.

I hadn't even caught her name, and yet the prospect of hanging out with her lingered in my thoughts like a catchy tune. The church faded into the background, and all I could think about was how my day had taken an unexpected turn.

Two hours into the long service, I was completely lost in my own thoughts when a loud yawn escaped my lips, echoing in the hushed sanctuary. A woman sitting in front of me turned around and shot me a glare that could've melted steel.

"Sorry," I said under my breath, sinking into my seat and wishing I could disappear. To my left, I spotted a balding, gray-haired man staring at me, his arms crossed like a disappointed school principal.

"Looks like someone was out late partying with the den of thieves last night," he said, his voice booming as he leaned closer. "You do know this is the house of God, don't you?"

I felt a surge of irritation rise within me, a desire to tell this old fool to mind his own business and leave me alone. But I bit my tongue; I had been taught to respect my elders, even if they rubbed me the wrong way. So instead, I forced a polite smile and settled deeper into my seat, reminding myself that I was here for a reason—just not one that seemed to matter much to him.

"I'm sorry, sir," I said, rubbing the tops of my legs as if that might soothe the tension in the air. "It won't happen again." I hoped my humble apology would soften him, but it only seemed to stoke his anger.

"The next time you feel the need to drag your tired butt into the house of the Lord," he said, loud enough for the people around us to hear, "don't."

"Yes, sir." I forced a tight smile, swallowing the comeback sitting on the tip of my tongue.

"Good." He stepped back, but his sharp eyes stayed locked on me, like he was daring me to mess up again.

Any chance of enjoying the service was gone. I felt like I was on trial, every move under his watchful glare. All I could think about now was how soon I could get out of here.

At 2:00 p.m., the choir returned to the stage for one final song before the altar call. My reason for attending had been to uncover the truth, but all I'd gotten was a lecture from a grumpy old man who treated me like a wayward kid. I sank into my seat, half-listening to the choir, already planning my escape. If I timed it right, I could make it out after the final hymn without anyone noticing.

When the service finally ended, I grabbed my Bible and made a beeline for the door, feeling like I'd wasted my afternoon. But just as I reached my truck, a familiar voice called out behind me. I turned, and there she was—the green-eyed beauty, walking toward me with a confidence that made her seem like she was gliding on air.

"You're not leaving without saying goodbye, are you?" she teased, her eyes sparkling with mischief.

Caught off guard, I blinked, momentarily distracted by the way her lips curved when she spoke. I realized too late that I'd been staring.

"My name is James," I finally said, awkwardly sticking out my hand like I was closing a business deal. "James Barnes."

She shook my hand with a light laugh. "Alexis Lee. Nice to meet you, James."

In what felt like seconds but could have been hours, we exchanged numbers and chatted about everything from her love of the Celtics and Patriots to her childhood in Connecticut. Her energy was contagious, and for the first time in what felt like forever, I wasn't thinking about Naomi. Alexis was vibrant, easy to talk to—she made me feel like I could finally exhale.

As we walked back toward the church, I caught myself grinning like a fool. Maybe this was exactly what I needed—a fresh start.

But just as we reached the edge of the parking lot, the low hum of a car engine caught my attention. A sleek black Audi R8 rolled up beside us, its dark-tinted windows giving nothing away. My stomach tightened as the driver's side window slid down.

And there she was.

*Naomi.*

# CHAPTER 30

*No one pours new wine into old wineskins*

OF ALL THE DAYS TO RUN INTO NAOMI, IT HAD TO BE today. My stomach did this weird turn, like I'd just stepped off a roller coaster I didn't want to be on. I was supposed to be forgetting her, moving on. But there she was—like some curse the universe decided to play on me.

Next to me, Alexis stood firm, her hand resting on my shoulder like a reminder to stay calm. "You good?" she asked, side-eyeing me like she already knew the answer.

"Yeah," I said, even though my voice cracked like a teenage boy's. Real convincing.

Out of the corner of my eye, I saw Naomi step out of her car, all confidence and grace, wearing a red dress that made it impossible to focus on anything else. I could even smell her perfume—subtle, but it hit like a punch to my chest. My mouth went dry.

"Brother James," she said, her voice a little too friendly as she locked her car. She turned toward me with a slow smile, the kind that could make a grown man forget his own name. "What brings you here today, stranger?"

I froze. My brain told my feet to move, but they weren't listening. She strolled toward me, heels clicking on the pavement like she was walking a runway. And me? I just stood there like a deer in headlights, praying Alexis didn't notice the beads of sweat forming on my forehead.

"Uh, hey, Naomi," I finally managed, my voice about two octaves too high. Smooth. Real smooth.

Naomi's eyes flicked to Alexis, then back to me, and that knowing smirk crept onto her face. I felt like I'd been caught with my hand in the cookie jar.

Alexis shifted beside me, and I could feel her glance, like she was silently saying, *Really, James?*

Before I could even register what was happening, Naomi's arms were around my neck, pulling me in so tightly it felt like our bodies were one. I could feel her heartbeat—or maybe it was mine, racing too fast to tell. "It's so good to see you," she whispered, her breath warm against my ear, leaving a sense of closeness that I hadn't expected.

It took me a moment to realize that Alexis was still standing there, watching this entire scene unfold with a polite smile—too polite. My brain scrambled, and I quickly let go of Naomi, stepping back as if I'd just touched something too hot.

I tried to play it cool, but the awkwardness was impossible to shake. Had I made it worse than it needed to be?

Clearing my throat, I shifted my attention back to Alexis. She was still smiling, but her eyes told a different story—one she wasn't saying out loud.

"Hey, Pastor," Alexis said with a bright smile, giving Naomi a quick hug. Without missing a beat, she slipped back to my side, casually looping her arm through mine like we were a couple who'd been together for years.

Naomi's face tightened as she looked between me and Alexis, her eyes narrowing just a little. She pressed her lips together before her gaze settled on me.

"So, I see you've met Brother James," Naomi said, her voice sharp, like she was fighting to stay calm.

"Yeah, we met today," Alexis replied, clearly enjoying herself. She leaned in just a little, her smile almost daring. "Turns out, we've got a lot in common. He's from Boston, I'm from

Connecticut. We're both diehard Patriots and Celtics fans. Practically neighbors."

Naomi's smile didn't quite reach her eyes. She studied me for a moment, her gaze sharp enough to make anyone uncomfortable. "Really?" she said, her tone flat. "Sister Alexis, do you mind if I have a word with Brother James... *alone?*"

I swallowed, feeling the tension build. *This can't end well,* I thought, hands shoved deep in my pockets, wishing I'd left the church service a few minutes earlier to avoid running into Naomi altogether. Of course, that would've been too easy—just my luck.

"Of course, Pastor," Alexis said smoothly. Then, without missing a beat, she slid her arms around my neck and gave me a quick kiss on the cheek, like a subtle reminder to Naomi about her place in my life. "We've got plans this week anyway," she added with a confident grin.

With a final smile, Alexis turned and walked back toward the church, her confidence impossible to ignore. I caught myself watching her a little too long. When I glanced up, Naomi was watching me, shaking her head like she'd just caught me sneaking out of church without putting anything in the offering plate.

Naomi opened the car door, eyes locking onto mine. "Get in," she said, her tone leaving no room for argument.

"But what about my truck parked around back?" I asked, like I needed her permission.

A voice inside my head told me to grow a pair, to take charge. But Naomi—she had a way of making me do what I didn't want to do. Or maybe I was just getting soft.

"I'll drive you," she said.

I hesitated. Part of me wanted to argue. The other part just wanted to get out of there and avoid whatever was coming next. I chose the easy route, walking around to the passenger side and sliding in like I was on punishment. I didn't even know what I'd done wrong, but it didn't matter.

The car felt suffocating, and I couldn't wait to get out. What happened to the Naomi I used to know? Or maybe the real question was, why had I even gotten in the car with her?

When we finally pulled up to my truck, I didn't hesitate. I muttered a quick thanks, got out, and fumbled to unlock my door. I could feel her eyes on me, but I didn't look back. I wasn't sure what I'd see if I did.

I climbed into my truck, still feeling the tension in the air. I thought I'd be able to shake it off once I drove away, but then my phone lit up on the seat next to me.

Naomi.

I stared at the screen, my thumb hovering over the accept button. Part of me wanted to just ignore it, keep driving, and forget about it. But something told me I couldn't. Not yet.

With a sigh, I tapped the screen and cleared my throat. "Hello?"

"We need to meet," she said, her voice steady, no softness, no hesitation—just a simple command that cut through the air.

For a moment, I just sat there, gripping the steering wheel, caught between logic and whatever the hell this was. Everything in me screamed to walk away, but something—some pull I couldn't ignore—told me I needed to hear her out. Maybe it was time to clear the air.

I didn't have anything else to do. But the pressure of the moment got the better of me. I didn't even think twice. "When and where?" I asked, my voice lower than usual, trying to sound like I had it together—even if I didn't.

"Your place. In two hours. See you soon."

Before I could even think to tell her my place wasn't the best choice, she hung up. I stared at the phone, unsure of what to do next. Naomi. At my place. This wasn't going to end well.

By the time I got home, the exhaustion of the day had settled in. Emotionally drained, I barely made it through the door before my phone buzzed again. I groaned inwardly. *Not now.*

I glanced at the screen. Alexis. *Of course.* I sighed and picked up, wondering how I'd ended up tangled in this mess.

"Hello?"

"Hey, James!" Alexis said, her voice upbeat. "It was great meeting you at church today. I'm excited to get to know you better. Let me know when you're free. The ball's in your court!"

Her enthusiasm hit me, but instead of lifting me up, it added weight. I felt like I was in the ring, getting hit from all sides. What was I doing? Why had I agreed to meet her when Naomi was still in my head, taking up way too much space? Naomi was everything I'd ever wanted—beautiful, captivating—but she was married. That should've been the end of it. But here I was, agreeing to meet Alexis, knowing nothing good would come of it.

And then there was Alexis— bright, upbeat, the kind of person I should be eager to get to know. But instead, I was stuck, caught between the past and the uncertainty of something new. *Was I just setting myself up for trouble?*

"Yeah," I said, my voice distant as I tried to pull myself together. "I'm looking forward to getting to know you, too. I'll send you my schedule later." I paused, trying to focus. "Actually, how about I take you to a Celtics game when they play the Wizards? You up for that?"

I threw the idea out there, trying to sound casual, like I had everything under control. But the truth? My head was a mess. Two hours until Naomi showed up, and now Alexis was on the line, all excited. What was I doing?

"Hell yeah!" Alexis practically shouted, then quickly switched gears. "I mean, yes, I'd love to go when the Celtics play the Wizards. I'll be waiting for your schedule. Have a great day, James. Go Pats!"

I chuckled, though my thoughts were already elsewhere. "OK, cool. Have a nice day," I said, hanging up. The moment the call ended, I felt it—the rush of tension, like I'd just stepped into a storm I couldn't avoid. Naomi was coming over. What had I agreed to?

I needed a strong drink to take the edge off. I grabbed the bourbon and a glass from the counter, pouring more than I probably should for 2:30 p.m. Leaning against the counter, I took a slow sip, letting the warmth spread through me. Was I looking for courage, or just trying to escape the mess I'd made? Either way, the bourbon was doing its job—until my phone buzzed.

I glanced at the screen. A text from Naomi.

I'm downstairs. Open the door. I'll be up in one minute.

One minute? Of course, she'd give me no time to prepare. My heart raced. I knocked back the rest of the bourbon and rushed to the bathroom. I brushed my teeth quickly, trying to get rid of any trace of the alcohol, gargled, and popped in a handful of mints just to be sure.

Then, the doorbell rang.

# CHAPTER 31

Resist the devil, and he will flee

"YOU'RE AFRAID OF ME, AREN'T YOU?" SHE SAID, marching right into the living room like she owned the place. She plopped herself dead center on the couch, crossed her legs, and stared at me with a smirk.

I just stood there, staring back, shaking my head. **Really?** She barges in, making herself at home, and now she thinks I'm scared? The audacity.

"Afraid of you?" I laughed as I made my way to the loveseat, sprawling out like I had all the time in the world. "Please, I've never been afraid of anyone. You? You're like the female Kevin Hart—tiny, loud, and full of jokes."

Her eyes widened for a split second; then, she let out a laugh. "Oh, you've got jokes now, huh?"

"I mean, if the shoe fits... not that you'd need a big size." I winked, dodging as she threw a pillow at me.

She shook her head, still smiling. "Keep talking. You're just trying to hide the fact that I'm in your head."

I leaned back, arms stretched over the loveseat. "Nah, the only thing you're in right now is my living room... uninvited, I might add."

What did she mean, *I'm afraid of her?* Who did this holy roller think she was talking to? I needed another drink, and fast. I headed to the kitchen, muttering under my breath, picturing something way stronger than bourbon that might actually make her logic make sense. If she was here to test my patience, she was doing a great job.

"Do you want anything to drink?" I called out, silently praying she wouldn't ask for more of my pricey champagne. After the Dom Pérignon fiasco, I'd learned the hard way to keep the good stuff out of sight. Note to self: find a better hiding spot.

"Yes," she replied, her voice suddenly way too close for comfort. When I spun around, there she was—standing inches away, smiling like she had something planned. She looked like a miniature statue, all calm and still, with a devilish grin that made me blink twice.

"What the heck!" I nearly jumped out of my skin. "You should never sneak up on people like that. You nearly scared the crap out of me!" My heart was pounding so hard it felt like it was about to break through my ribcage. I'd heard stories about the Holy Ghost *carrying* someone, but this felt like a scene straight out of *The Exorcist.*

She slapped me on the back, laughing way too loud for my nerves. "See? I *told* you you're afraid of me!"

I shook my head, letting out a slow breath to steady myself, then reached for a glass. "Here we go again," I muttered, grabbing the bottle of Jose Cuervo. I held it up, glancing her way. "Drink? Snack? Your call."

"What do you have?" she asked, pulling open the refrigerator with the kind of ease that made it look like she belonged here. She leaned against the doorframe, scanning the shelves like a detective solving a case. "When was the last time you had a home-cooked meal?" Her gaze shifted to me, eyes full of judgment. "All I see are boxes of leftovers. Guess I was right about you."

*Right about me?* What was that supposed to mean? Since she seemed to be playing some kind of game, I figured I'd play along. If she wanted to throw shade, I'd throw it right back.

"Well," I said, sitting on a stool at the bar and leaning my elbows on the counter. "Since you know so much about me, how about you cook me a real meal?"

Her lips curled into a sly smile as she silently closed the refrigerator door and strolled back to the living room. I watched, wondering what she was up to. Moments later, she appeared in the kitchen doorway again, her purse slung over her shoulder and car keys dangling in her hand like a prize.

Without so much as a glance in my direction, she turned on her heels and walked straight out the front door. Not a single goodbye, no witty remark—just gone.

I sat there, staring at the door for a second, wondering what game she was playing now. And why, despite everything, it felt like she was winning.

*What just happened?* I thought, staring out of the living room window, watching her car pull away. *Was it something I said or did?* For a moment, I wondered, but quickly brushed it off. *No, this wasn't my problem—it was hers.* Women could be so unpredictable. Maybe her storming out was actually a blessing in disguise. I grabbed my glass of tequila and sank into the couch, ready to watch the late afternoon football game.

Still, the thought lingered. *What just happened?* Did asking her to make me a home-cooked meal really cause her to run off like that?

About an hour later, a soft knock on the front door pulled me from my thoughts. *Who* could that be? I peered through the blinds with just my fingers, and sure enough, Naomi's car was back in the same spot as before. *Of course.*

I tiptoed to the front door and leaned in to check through the peephole.

"Open the door, James," her voice came through, light and teasing. "I know you're standing there. I can hear you breathing."

Great, I thought, caught.

I couldn't help but chuckle quietly to myself as I slowly opened the door. Before I could even say a word, she barged in like a whirlwind, pushing me aside and heading straight for the kitchen, her arms loaded with two grocery bags.

"You asked for a home-cooked meal," she said, unpacking the bags with focus, pulling out ingredients one by one. "So, a home-cooked meal you'll have. You know, like the Bible says, ask, and you shall receive."

I stood there, blinking, watching her rummage through my cupboards with a determination that made me feel like I was the one who needed to get out of her way. This cannot be happening, I thought, but it clearly was. She was already grabbing a large pot, a pan, and any cooking utensil she could find.

"Where are your seasonings?" she asked, not even bothering to turn around.

"They're in that spice tray to the right. I think it's called a lazy Susan?"

She burst out laughing and glanced over her shoulder. "Typical man," she said, shaking her head as she grabbed a handful of spices.

"What's that supposed to mean?" I asked, crossing my arms and watching her.

"Salt, pepper, garlic powder, and Lowry's? This barely counts as seasoning," she said, still laughing as she filled the pot with water and set it on the stove. "You really need a woman in your life. And not just any woman," she added, tossing me a look. "A good woman. A woman handpicked by God."

I raised an eyebrow, feeling like I'd just been hit with a backhanded compliment. Maybe Naomi had a point. I hadn't been in a serious relationship in years. Maybe it was time to settle down with "a good woman," as she put it. Alexis came to mind. We had a lot in common—same sports teams, easy on the eyes, and she was God-fearing. It made sense. I could see the benefits of being in a relationship. But then again... I'd lose my privacy.

I could already picture it: being told when to come home, not to leave my shoes in the middle of the floor, and getting side-eyed every time I spent money on something that wasn't "necessary." My bachelor pad? Forget it. It would turn into a flowery, pastel-scented haze, with decorative pillows and bathroom sets that matched. The thought gave me pause, and before I found myself mentally picking out bedspreads, I quickly switched gears.

"So, what's on the menu?" I asked, trying to steer the conversation away from my potential loss of freedom.

"Listen, mister," Naomi said, grabbing my hand and pulling me out of the kitchen like I was some helpless bystander. She shoved me onto the couch, snatched the remote from the coffee table, and flashed me a look. "I've got this. You just enjoy the game. I'll call you if I need anything. And stay out of the kitchen if you know what's good for you."

I raised my hands in mock surrender. "Yes, boss!"

Settling onto the couch with the remote in hand, I glanced toward the kitchen where the sound of clanging pots and pans filled the air. A grin tugged at my lips—maybe having Naomi around wasn't so bad after all.

Propping my feet up on the coffee table, I took a slow sip of tequila and turned my attention to the second half of the Patriots game. My smile deepened when I heard Naomi humming *Victory* by Yolanda Adams from the kitchen. For the first time in what felt like forever, it was nice to feel looked after.

As the game played on, my thoughts drifted back to the idea of being in a relationship. Maybe this kind of life wouldn't be so bad.

About twenty minutes later, the smell coming from the kitchen had my stomach growling. "Whatever you're cooking smells amazing!" I called, trying not to sound too eager.

Naomi never ceased to surprise me. Smart, beautiful, a natural leader—and now, she could cook too? Was there anything she couldn't do?

"You'll see," she called back.

By the time the third quarter rolled around, Naomi walked into the living room wearing a bright apron that said, "Master Chef." Where had that even come from? Maybe she grabbed it with the groceries. Either way, she looked great in it—too great.

I wasn't sure if it was the tequila or just my long stretch of being single, but for a split second, I forgot she was married. The thought disappeared as quickly as it had come, snapping me back to reality.

"Where would you like to eat?" she asked, breaking my thoughts.

"I usually just eat on the couch in front of the TV," I admitted, suddenly feeling a little self-conscious. "It's just me, after all."

"Well, not tonight," she said firmly,. "We're eating at that gorgeous dining table of yours. I've already set the placemats, and I'm using your nice silverware and those fancy plates. No more paper plates and plastic forks—you're a king, and it's time you're treated like one."

A smile crept onto my face. No one had ever called me a king before. It felt... good. Without a word, I made my way to the dining room like an obedient soldier.

"I like a man who follows orders," she teased with a giggle as she disappeared back into the kitchen.

A moment later, she returned, carrying a basket of warm dinner rolls, a bottle of wine, and two glasses. As she poured the wine into my glass, her eyes lingered on mine.

"We're making a toast tonight," she said with a knowing smile.

I held back a laugh, thinking, *Hopefully, after you do the dishes.*

"What's the occasion?" I asked, eyeing the expensive bottle of wine. *How had she even found my stash?*

"Be patient, honey," she replied, disappearing into the kitchen again.

*Honey?* The word threw me, sending a warning signal through my brain. This felt like playing with fire.

When she returned, she carried a tray with two covered plates. My curiosity peaked as she set them on the table. Rubbing my hands together, I couldn't wait to see what she'd cooked up.

"I really appreciate you cooking for me," I said, slipping the napkin onto my lap as she placed the plate in front of me.

"I hope you like filet mignon, oven-roasted asparagus, and homemade garlic mashed potatoes," she said with a smile that could melt steel.

As I lifted the lid, the aroma hit me like a tidal wave, and my stomach growled in response. This was far beyond anything I'd expected.

"You made all this for me?" I asked, happier than a pig at feeding time. Everything looked perfect, and I could barely resist diving in. "No one's ever cooked me a meal like this. Thank you."

"It won't be the last time, sweetheart," she said, her eyes sparkling with something warm, something magnetic.

When our eyes met, a fire lit inside me—a spark I hadn't felt in years, one I couldn't ignore. Before I even realized it, the words slipped out.

*"I think I love you, Naomi."*

Her face softened, her eyes lighting up like flickering candles.

"Really?" she asked gently, reaching across the table to hold my hands. *"I love you too, James."*

Her voice carried an emotion so raw, so unguarded, it seemed like she'd been waiting to say it for an eternity.

"Kiss me," she whispered, her gaze locking onto mine.

*Wait, what?* My mind reeled as I snapped back to reality. *What had I just done?*

Panic set in as my words lingered, uninvited and undeniable. This was Naomi—married, unavailable, and completely off-limits. Had I really just let that slip?

The world around me blurred. It felt as though time had slowed, trapping me in the moment. I searched her face, desperate for any sign of hesitation or even confusion. Instead, her beautiful smile stayed firmly in place, radiating warmth.

But that smile only made my dread sink deeper.

# CHAPTER 32

*Nothing in all creation is hidden from God*

AFTER DINNER, I FELT LIKE I WAS SITTING ON A LIVE grenade; thanks to that accidental *I love you* I'd blurted out. Naomi was still sitting across from me, smiling like everything was fine, while my brain screamed, *abort mission!* Every time her eyes lingered on mine, it felt like we were inching closer to the danger zone—my bedroom.

I could practically see it happening: us swapping spit, tangled in sheets, and me trying to explain why the ten commandments suddenly didn't apply. Nope, that's not happening. Adultery wasn't on my to-do list.

I cleared my throat, shifting awkwardly in my chair, glancing at the clock as if I had somewhere important to be. My mind raced, desperately trying to come up with an excuse, any excuse, to get her out of my house before things got messy—literally and figuratively. Maybe I'd say I had an early meeting. Or better yet, a "surprise plumbing emergency."

I had to get her out of here fast.

"That was the best meal I've ever had," I said, quickly grabbing the dishes and hurrying them into the kitchen like I was trying to flee the scene of a crime. "I don't know where you learned to cook like that, but you've got some serious skills. You can cook for me anytime."

*There I go again,* I thought, mentally facepalming. At this rate, I was putting my foot in my mouth faster than Usain Bolt could finish a sprint.

"How can I repay you for such an amazing meal?" I asked, bracing myself for her answer. After all, this was Naomi we were talking about—an unpredictable woman of God with surprises up her sleeve.

"Well," she said, joining me in the kitchen with that sly smile of hers. "I still have room for dessert."

"Dessert?" I blinked. *Who buys groceries, cooks a five-star meal for a king—no pun intended—and forgets dessert?* I had to hand it to her; she was good. Real good.

Naomi stepped closer, her smile never fading. She tilted her head. "Dessert, James. You know, the part that comes after dinner?" Her tone was playful, daring me to keep up.

I swallowed hard, suddenly aware of how close she was standing. My mind raced, but it was completely blank—of *course, I knew what dessert was*, but now, under her gaze, I felt like a deer caught in headlights.

The kitchen around me felt suddenly too small, and I glanced around, hoping for some kind of inspiration. Her eyes were still on me, waiting. My palms felt a little sweaty, and I could feel the tension in the air as my mind scrambled. *Think, think, think!* Then, like a switch being flipped, an idea flashed in my head. A grin slowly spread across my face. *Saved.*

*Shindigz.*

"I know a spot about fifteen minutes away that'll change the way you think about dessert," I said, leaning in with a smirk. "Trust me." I grabbed my keys off the counter, twirling them between my fingers. "What do you say -up for a little adventure?"

Naomi laughed, shaking her head. "A king, huh? Alright, I'm in." She grabbed her purse and threw me a playful look. "Lead the way."

As we walked out, she slipped her arm through mine without a second thought. It was easy, familiar—like we'd done it a hundred times before.

The truck beeped as I hit the unlock button, the sound crisp in the quiet night. Without hesitation, I walked Naomi to the passenger side and pulled the door open, straightening my posture like I actually knew what I was doing. "Your chariot awaits," I said, throwing in a wink for good measure.

Naomi smirked, sliding into the seat with effortless grace. "I see chivalry isn't dead," she teased, adjusting her purse in her lap.

I eased the door shut, pausing just a second to make sure she was comfortable before heading around to the driver's side, forcing an air of confidence I didn't actually have. Truth was, I had no clue where we were going.

I slid behind the wheel, buckled up, and turned the key.

*BOOM.*

Nipsey Hussle's *Racks in the Middle* exploded through the speakers, shaking the truck. My hand shot to the volume knob, twisting frantically as my pulse jumped. Naomi raised an eyebrow, clearly amused. Meanwhile, I was busy praying she wouldn't revoke my gentleman status over a not-so-holy playlist.

Before I could reach the dial, her hand landed on my arm, gentle but firm. "This is your truck, James. Play whatever you want."

I blinked. That caught me off guard. Holy roller or not, I figured rap music would be an automatic no-go. But then—she started nodding along, even mouthing a few of the lyrics. I watched for a second, half convinced I'd slipped into an alternate reality.

Grinning, I cranked the volume back up, threw the truck into drive, and hit the road. Maybe this night was about to get a whole lot more interesting.

Fifteen minutes later, I pulled up outside *Shindigz*, one of Richmond's top dessert spots—home of the kind of sweets that made people forget about diets. I had no doubt Naomi would be impressed.

I cut the engine, hopped out, and circled to her side, pulling the door open. She swung her legs out smoothly, and as I helped her down, her fingers slid into mine like it was the most natural thing in the world.

"You keep treating me like this," she said, flashing a smile, "and you'll have me eating out of your hands."

I swallowed hard, completely defenseless against her words. If only she knew—I wanted her eating off more than just my hands. She was my kryptonite, and I didn't stand a chance.

Trying to pull it together, I slid a hand around her waist and led her inside. The air was thick with the scent of sugar and va-nilla, the kind of warmth that wrapped around you like a hug. Naomi's eyes lit up as she took in the pastries behind the glass, her lips parting just slightly in delight. Yeah, I'd definitely scored points tonight.

Even if, deep down, I knew we could never really be.

"You're gonna love this place," I said as we stepped up to the counter.

A petite woman with short dreadlocks greeted us with a bright smile. "Welcome to Shindigz."

Naomi's eyes lit up as she took in the desserts behind the glass. Then, out of nowhere, she leaned up and kissed my cheek.

"This place is amazing," she whispered before turning to the cashier. "I'll have whatever he's having."

I grinned, stepping up to place the order. "We'll take a half slice of the Spotted Cow and a half slice of the fresh fruit cake, with two lattes," I said confidently, knowing she'd appreciate me taking charge.

The woman nodded. "Great choices."

After paying, we took a seat outside.

A few minutes later, a blue-eyed guy with a buzz cut strolled over, balancing our plates like a pro.

"Enjoy," he said with a grin before heading back inside.

Naomi reached for my hands. "Let's pray."

I laced my fingers through hers and closed my eyes—until a deep rumble cut through the air. The low growl of engines grew louder, vibrating through the pavement.

I cracked one eye open as a group of motorcycles pulled up along the side street.

Black leather. Heavy boots. Like something straight out of an action movie.

Then, the last guy took off his helmet.

*Bryce.*

# CHAPTER 33



MY STOMACH TIGHTENED THE SECOND I SAW BRYCE. Here? At the same restaurant? At the same time? The odds felt too slim, like something bigger was at play—something with a sense of humor. Maybe this was God's way of yanking the rug out from under us, making sure the truth got out, since we couldn't keep it under wraps ourselves.

I shifted in my seat, my throat dry, as if the very air in the room had thickened. The thought of Bryce walking over, eyes narrowing as he put two and two together, made my heart pound so hard I could practically hear it. I wiped my palms on my jeans, trying to play it cool. But inside, I was one wrong look away from bolting for the door.

But then again, it wasn't like Bryce ever *said* Naomi was his wife. Sure, they had the same last name, and yeah, he wore that wedding ring like it meant something, but that didn't prove anything.

I swallowed hard, my mind racing to stitch together any excuse for what he might see, but none of them were good. Betting on this situation to somehow work itself out? No thanks. I wasn't taking that gamble.

Panic surged through me as I realized I had seconds to think fast, or else I'd find myself toe-to-toe with the four of them. I didn't need a calculator to figure out my odds of winning that face-off—zero. Zilch. Spinning around, I faced the wall, my heart pounding like I'd just sprinted a mile. I felt like a straight-up punk. Here I was, out with a married woman, and now I was hiding like some kid caught sneaking candy.

God saw everything, of course—no dodging that—but somehow, I was more worried about hiding from these people than from Him. Brilliant logic, right?

As their footsteps got closer to the entrance, I grabbed Naomi's hand and, without thinking, kissed it. A distraction, a move, something to shift the attention.

Her cheeks flushed a soft pink. "*What was that for?*"

I cleared my throat, trying to stay cool. "I just think you're the bomb," I said, my voice smooth enough—never mind the fact that my pulse was going haywire.

I stole a glance over my shoulder as the group of four strolled into Shindigz. This wasn't what I expected. Not even close.

"And I have a surprise for you," I blurted out before I could stop myself.

*A surprise?* Seriously? Where the hell did that come from?

My brain scrambled for an escape route as I realized I'd just dug myself into a hole so deep, they could bury me standing. My throat went dry. Heat coiled in my stomach. This was heading into dangerous territory fast.

Desperate, I grabbed my latte and took a sip, hoping it would ground me.

Instead, my face twisted in disgust.

"This is terrible," I blurted out, putting the cup down like it had personally offended me.

"Want me to get you a new one?" she offered, standing up before I could stop her.

"No, no!" I panicked, nearly sloshing the latte all over my shirt. "I got this."

In my rush to escape, I spun too fast, abandoning the cursed drink on the table.

I exhaled, thinking I had a moment to breathe—until I glanced back. Naomi was already strolling toward the entrance, latte in hand, her bright smile lighting up her face. My stomach dropped.

At the counter, Bryce and his boys scanned the menu, oblivious. But not for long.

"You forgot your latte, silly!" Naomi called out, somehow louder than the music pumping through the speakers.

Heads turned. Bryce's crew included.

Before their eyes could fully lock on me, I lunged, shoving Naomi back out the door, nearly splashing her with the latte in the process.

"It's not that bad," I muttered, downing the drink like my life depended on it. "Ahhhhhh."

Wiping foam from my mouth, I forced a grin.

Naomi folded her arms, giving me a long, suspicious look. "Are you sure you're okay?" Her eyes darted past me toward the restaurant entrance. "You're not hiding from someone, are you?"

"Yes—I mean, no!" My voice cracked. I scrambled for my keys, nearly knocking them off the table before snatching them up. "Can we just… go?"

"Not until you tell me what's going on," she said, suspicion sharpening her tone.

My pulse kicked into overdrive as Bryce and his crew headed for the exit, my brain scrambling for an escape. *Think. Move. Do something!* But I was frozen, trapped in the worst possible moment.

Then, as if the universe hadn't tormented me enough, an all-too-familiar hum of an engine sent ice down my spine. My head snapped toward the entrance just in time to see a red BMW roll up.

No way. No way this was happening to me tonight.

My stomach bottomed out as Alexis stepped out of the car. This had to be some kind of cosmic punishment for messing around with a married woman. The universe wasn't just stacking the deck against me—it was shuffling, cutting, and dealing me a losing hand.

My mind screamed for me to abandon ship, leave Naomi standing there, and get in my car— no explanations, no good-byes. Just floor it and don't look back.

But before I could follow through on that escape plan, my feet betrayed me, dragging me toward the parking lot. Each step felt heavy, like I was walking into a storm I couldn't outrun. The rubber was about to meet the road in the worst possible way.

And right there, caught in the chaos, with nowhere left to turn, I did the one thing I never saw coming.

I prayed.

"God, I'm in a mess, and I need you to get me out of it," I muttered under my breath, eyes squeezed shut. "I know I'm probably not your favorite child, but if you pull me through this, I promise I'll try to stick to the straight and narrow. No more detours, no more wide roads. Just... help me out of this mess. In Jesus' name, amen."

When I opened my eyes, it felt like something out of a movie. Bryce had spotted Alexis and was already chatting with her by her car, laughing like they were old friends. The two of them were so absorbed in conversation, they didn't notice anything else around them.

I blinked, hardly believing my luck. This was my golden moment. There was no way I was sticking around to see how it played out. I spun on my heel and slipped out of the parking lot like a man who'd just dodged a bullet.

This was my chance to escape.

"Mind if we take the food back to my place?" I asked, trying to sound casual, though my nerves were hanging by a thread. Naomi shot me a glance from the corner of her eye—she wasn't happy. Not at all. But at that point, I didn't care. I just needed to get out of there before things went from bad to worse.

I knew Shindigz was popular, but not *this* popular. Lesson learned—Naomi and I wouldn't be coming back.

"Of course, we can," she said, voice tight as she grabbed her purse. We slipped out quietly, keeping a safe distance from Bryce and Alexis, who were still deep in conversation. My heart pounded with every step, but somehow, we made it to my truck without incident.

Once inside, I didn't bother with my seatbelt. I peeled out of the parking lot like I was making a getaway in a heist movie. The second we hit the main road, relief crashed over me. It felt like I'd just won the lottery. God had come through—again.

Merging onto the highway, I glanced at Naomi, who was still watching me with that same unreadable expression. Shaking my head, I let out a quiet laugh at the absurdity of it all.

"God, I owe you one," I said under my breath, still amazed I'd managed to slip away before things got messy.

# CHAPTER 34

*Free your mind*

IT WAS 9:30 P.M. WHEN I PULLED UP TO MY APARTMENT, feeling like I'd been carrying a load I had no business shouldering. I couldn't believe it—avoiding Bryce like I was some kind of fugitive. How did it even come to this? All I wanted was the truth, *but was it even my truth to tell?*

I was supposed to have it all together—a successful, single guy who had his life mapped out. Or at least, that's what I told myself. But everything shifted the night I walked into that church and locked eyes with Naomi. That's when the compass spun out of control.

I stepped out of the truck and rounded the front to open Naomi's door. Just as I reached her, the sky opened up, rain pouring down. But I barely felt it—my mind was too tangled in thoughts to notice. For a second, I felt completely lost, wandering with no direction, and I had no one to blame but myself.

I reached for the handle—*click*. I froze. Had she just locked the door?

"You have to be kidding me," I thought, already done with the games. Naomi waved from behind the window, motioning for me to get back inside, but I wasn't having it. I yanked the handle, tried the key—nothing. Just that same mocking *click* every time.

Suddenly, my phone buzzed in my pocket, making me jump. My mind raced—Bryce? Alexis? What if one of them was calling to question why I was at Shindigz with Naomi, a married woman? This couldn't be good.

I exhaled sharply, pulled out my phone, and stared at the screen. Naomi?

Confused, I glanced toward the car and saw her sitting comfortably inside, phone pressed to her ear. I answered. "Why are you calling me?"

She gave me a look through the windshield like the answer was obvious. "It's raining," she said. "And you know good and well a Black woman with straightened hair and water do not mix. You trying to have me out here looking like a Chia Pet?"

She smiled, and despite myself, I cracked a grin as she handed me a pink handkerchief, her perfume still lingering on it.

"Thanks," I said, shaking my head. The thought of her hair meeting the rain nearly made me laugh—one second sleek and perfect, the next a full-blown afro. "You're funny."

Before I could dwell on it, her hand rested lightly on mine. "I know you're battling between good and evil, James," she said, her voice quiet but sure.

Something about the way she said it made me feel exposed, like she could see straight into my heart. But I didn't want comfort—I wanted the truth.

"Can I ask you something?" I turned to her, our eyes locking.

"Anything," she said without hesitation. "No lies. Whatever you want to know."

I nodded, bracing myself for whatever came next. Just as I opened my mouth, my phone rang, slicing through the moment like a knife.

Not again, I thought, glancing at the screen.

Bryce.

**Busted**. I quickly placed my hand over the screen to keep Naomi from seeing who was calling. Out of my peripheral, I caught her staring—first at me, then the phone, then back at me. Panicking wouldn't help, so I forced a casual smile, hoping to divert her attention. But as the buzzing continued, she raised an eyebrow.

"So you're not gonna answer that, huh?"

"They'll leave a message," I said, my voice a little too tight, like I'd just been caught with my hand in the cookie jar.

"But it could be important."

I shrugged. "You have my undivided attention, so all calls go to voicemail."

Naomi folded her arms. "What if it's your mom?"

She had me there. I hesitated for a second, gripping the wheel, then shook my head. "She'd text if it was serious."

She didn't look convinced, but after a moment, she sighed. "Okay, but don't blame me if it was important."

I kept my eyes on the road, but my mind spun in circles. Bryce. Naomi. That phone call. If I had nothing to worry about, why did it feel like I was running? Why was I avoiding the one question that could settle everything?

**Do you know Bryce Adams?**

It was simple. Direct. But I couldn't bring myself to say it. Maybe I didn't want to know the answer. Maybe knowing meant accepting the truth —and once I did, there'd be no hiding from the mess I'd made.

The phone had stopped buzzing, but in my head, the questions wouldn't.

When we finally made it back to my apartment, I wasn't in the mood for a nightcap. I walked Naomi to her car, offering a half-hearted smile as she slid into the driver's seat. She hesitated, like she wanted to say something, but instead, she just nodded. I stepped back, watching as her taillights disappeared into the night.

Alone now, I exhaled, but the unease remained. I had dodged questions all night—mostly from myself. And the worst part? I wasn't sure I wanted the answers.

# CHAPTER 35

*Seek first his kingdom and his righteousness*

A FEW DAYS LATER, I STUMBLED OUT OF GOLD'S GYM, muscles aching from a brutal full-body workout. The sunlight was blinding, forcing me to squint as I stepped outside. As I reached for my keys, my phone vibrated in my pocket.

*Alexis.*

Until now, we'd only exchanged short, casual texts, so seeing her name pop up on my screen caught me off guard. And right now, I could use the distraction.

I hesitated, wiping sweat from my forehead, then swiped to answer.

"Hello," I said, aiming for casual, but my voice dropped lower, like a bad radio announcer.

"This is James."

I always found it strange that I felt the need to announce myself whenever someone called, as if they wouldn't recognize my voice or, worse, had dialed the wrong number.

Seconds later, her voice filled the line, cutting through my thoughts.

"Please tell me that's not your official phone greeting," she laughed. "I mean, I know who I'm calling—I have your number and a picture of your handsome face saved in my phone! Just do the world a favor and stick to a simple 'hello,' okay?"

She laughed again, and I couldn't help but grin at her teasing. *Wait—picture?*

Where had she gotten a photo of me? Had I been careless enough to send her one? No, that didn't seem right. Then it hit me—she must've snapped a quick shot while I was running around the church like a clumsy toddler.

Alexis, Alexis, Alexis," I practically sang her name as I merged onto West Broad Street. "This is a surprise. What's up?"

The question felt dumb as soon as I said it. I'd just seen her at Shindigz, cozying up with Bryce. Was this call about that? Had she spotted Naomi and me huddled together like a couple of lovebirds? Was she about to blow my cover?

"You got plans tonight?" Alexis asked. "Texting all the time is for the birds. I can't really get to know you through a screen. There's more to you than just running around the church, right?" She laughed.

The only plans I had were sinking into the couch with a bowl of popcorn, watching a college football game in the afternoon, then catching the Celtics-Wizards matchup later that night. Not exactly thrilling. But after the week I'd had, it sounded perfect.

"Nothing major," I said. "Why, what's up?"

"I was hoping you'd say that," she said, a grin in her voice. "I scored two tickets to the Wizards game tonight."

"No way," I said, inching forward in the long drive-thru line. "How'd you get those?"

"My friend works at Capital One," she said. "She invited me, but something came up, so…"

"So… what?" I leaned in, already knowing where this was going but wanting to hear her say it.

Right then, a cheerful Chick-fil-A worker walked up to my car, her smile bright enough to light up the whole drive-thru.

"Well, I was hoping maybe you would—"

"Yes!" I blurted before she could finish. "I'd love to go!"

"Welcome to Chick-fil-A!" The blue-eyed attendant smiled. "Can I get a name for the order?"

"James."

"How can I serve you today?"

"I'll have a twelve-count nugget meal, large fries, and a Coke with light ice. No sauces."

"Will that complete your order?"

I nodded and handed her my credit card, grinning—more excited about the game tonight than the friendly service.

"Here's your receipt. Have a great day!"

"Thank you!" I called out to the freckled teen.

"My pleasure!" she replied, already greeting the next car.

I rolled up the window, unmuted my phone, and pulled into the pickup line.

"Sorry about that!" I said to Alexis. "Took longer than I thought."

"No problem, Handsome," she teased. I could almost picture her smirking. "Patience is one of my better qualities. I was mul-titasking anyway."

"Good to know," I said, feeling a bit humbled. A patient wom-an was exactly what I needed in my life right now.

"So, it's a date?"

"A date?" I echoed, scrambling to catch up.

"For the basketball game tonight, silly," she teased. "And for the record, it is a date."

"Absolutely, it's a date," I said, aiming for cool but probably sounding too eager. The clock on my Apple CarPlay read 11:05 a.m. "What time should I be ready?"

"Let's plan to leave around three. That work?"

"It does."

"Great!" Her excitement matched mine. "Text me your home address."

Wait, what? My stomach dropped. The last thing I needed was Alexis showing up at my apartment unannounced. I could barely handle Naomi crossing boundaries I hadn't even set. Fool me once, shame on you. Fool me twice? That was on me.

"What kind of man would I be if I let you pick me up?" I laid the chivalry on thick, hoping she'd buy it. "Send me your address. I'll be there at 2:55."

"Deal," she said. "Sending it now."

A moment later, my phone chimed, and her address popped up on the screen.

"Got it," I said, pulling into my parking spot. "See you at 2:55."

"See you then," she replied, and we hung up.

Within ten minutes, I was parked in front of my apartment, grinning like a fat kid with a giant piece of cake. Alexis inviting me to an NBA game felt like an honor—especially since it was the Boston Celtics, my favorite team. Despite the rough start to my day, things were turning out a lot better than I'd expected.

This was a good thing, right?

Chick-fil-A bag and Coke in hand, I took the stairs two at a time. For the first time in a while, it felt like things were finally shifting in my favor. God knows I needed it.

# CHAPTER 36

*I am doing a new thing*

DRESSED IN MY CUSTOM BLACK AND GREEN BOSTON Celtics Nike sweatsuit, a crisp white tee, and matching Jordans, I looked every bit like one of the players. I was thankful I'd gotten a fresh haircut a few days earlier. Surely, I was going to turn heads.

After locking Alexis' address into the GPS, I glanced at the single red rose on the passenger seat and grinned. A simple touch, but it felt right. Tonight was going to be something special. I could feel it.

Pulling out of the apartment complex, I turned the dial, scrolling past my usual rap stations before settling on a Gospel station. After what happened with Naomi, I wasn't about to go down that road with Alexis—though she probably wouldn't have minded.

Exactly twelve minutes later, I pulled into a gated community where every house screamed half a million dollars or more. The kind of place where the lawns were manicured to perfection, and even the air smelled expensive.

It hit me then—I had no idea what Alexis did for a living. Whatever it was, it had to pay well for her to be living like this.

I lowered the stereo volume, not wanting to stand out or give one of her nosy neighbors a reason to call the cops on the "strange Black man" rolling through their quiet, pristine neighborhood. The last thing I needed was to end up on the front page of the *Richmond Times-Dispatch*, or worse—on the wrong side of a racist cop's gun.

Turning slowly onto Florida Street, I spotted her house right away. There, sitting in the driveway, was her red two-door BMW, complete with the custom license plate: *Gods Grl*.

Pulling in behind her sleek BMW, I popped a few Altoids, making sure my breath was minty fresh. I grabbed the single red rose from the passenger seat and stepped out of the truck like I was about to pick up Cinderella herself.

As I walked up the long driveway, I couldn't help but notice how the grass was a flawless shade of green, like something out of a home improvement magazine. The flower beds were perfectly lined with tulips and some other flowers I couldn't name. I had the sudden urge to pluck one, but common sense kicked in—plus, her neighbors were probably watching.

Ascending the few steps to her front door, I mentally coached myself on how I'd greet her. But why was I nervous? This wasn't even a real date, just two friends heading to a game. Still, my heart raced like I was standing outside before prom night, about to meet her four-hundred-pound father.

The porch light flickered on, and I heard the doorknob turn.

*Breathe, James,* I muttered under my breath—accidentally louder than I'd intended.

The door swung open, and there she was, looking like she'd stepped straight out of a sports fan's dream. She wore a black and green Jason Tatum jersey, a fitted black baseball cap with "CELTICS" emblazoned across the front in bold green letters, and blue jeans that hugged her figure just right. To top it off, she had on a pair of Timberland boots—the same style I wore the first time I visited her church.

Nice touch.

"2:55 on the dot," Alexis said, flashing a perfect smile. "Impressive. And I like your outfit, too."

"You look amazing," I replied, pulling the rose from behind my back and handing it to her. "And I especially like those boots."

She took the rose, bringing it to her nose for a soft inhale. "I love roses. Thank you, James," she said, her eyes bright. "And I wore these boots just for *you.*"

She reached up and wrapped her arms around my neck, hugging me in a way that felt... right. Her scent hit me—orange blossom with something sweet, like white chocolate. It was intoxicating.

"Thanks for agreeing to hang out with me tonight," she said, her voice smooth, almost musical.

As we stood there, holding each other a little longer than expected, I leaned in closer, my lips near her ear. "I'm looking forward to tonight, Alexis."

"Me too," she whispered back.

But just as the moment started to feel like something straight out of a movie, a voice rang out.

"Hey, Alexis!"

I pulled back slightly, turning to see an older white woman power-walking alongside another woman pushing a baby stroller. Both were staring right at us, one of them waving enthusiastically—like they'd just caught us doing something.

Alexis let out a small sigh but waved back politely. "Those are my nosy neighbors," she muttered through a tight-lipped smile. "Hi, Doris! Getting your steps in, I see."

Without hesitation, Doris and her stroller-pushing friend veered straight toward us, all smiles, clearly not planning to let us escape without a little chat.

"And where are you two off to?" Doris asked, eyeing me like I was the main course at Sunday dinner. "And who's this handsome gentleman?"

"This is my friend, James," Alexis said smoothly, though I caught her sneaking a side-eye at me, amused. "We're heading to D.C. for the Wizards game."

"Well, it's a pleasure, James!" Before I could even extend my hand, Doris lunged forward and pulled me into a hug—and then, out of nowhere, her hand landed right on my backside.

"Whoa!" I jumped back, nearly tripping over the curb. What just happened?

Doris, completely unfazed, gave an approving nod to her blonde friend. "It's firm."

The blonde smirked and nodded back as if they'd just confirmed some important fact.

"Well, we won't keep you kids," Doris added, throwing in a wink—like she hadn't just crossed every personal boundary known to man. "Have a nice time!"

"Thanks, Doris." Alexis barely held in her laughter until they were a safe distance away, but then it spilled out in full.

I stood there, still processing what had just happened. "You know she grabbed my—"

"Welcome to the neighborhood," Alexis chuckled, playfully nudging me as we headed toward my truck. "You'll get used to it."

I shook my head, still laughing despite myself. "I don't know if I'm ready for that kind of warm welcome."

As I opened the passenger door for her, she shot me a teasing grin. "Well, consider it an initiation."

"Yeah, some initiation," I smiled, climbing into the driver's seat. But hey, at least the night was off to an interesting start.

# CHAPTER 37

*Save me from liars and deceivers*

WALKING INTO CAPITAL ONE ARENA FELT ELECTRIC. THE energy in the air was unreal, buzzing all around us before we even made it to our seats. The smell of buttered popcorn mixed with the faint scent of beer, and everywhere we looked, there were fans decked out in red, white, and blue jerseys. No doubt about it—we were deep in enemy territory.

Alexis and I, rocking our Celtics gear from head to toe, might as well have been waving a giant Come at us sign. As we followed the usher to our seats, a few Wizards fans gave us polite smiles, but others looked at us like, *Y'all sure you're in the right place?*

I glanced around, taking in the arena—the polished court, the massive video boards flashing player stats, the hype music pumping through the speakers. Say what you want about the Wizards, but they knew how to put on a show.

Our seats weren't courtside like the ones I got when Will hooked me up for that Celtics-Lakers game, but they were solid—mid-level, great view, close enough to feel part of the action but far enough from the nosebleeds to breathe easy.

As soon as we sat down, Alexis leaned over with a smirk. "You know if the Celtics win, we might not make it out of here in one piece, right?"

I smirked back, glancing at the row of diehard Wizards fans next to us—one of them already rolling their eyes. "Let 'em try," I said under my breath. "We came to see the Celtics win, and I'm not about to apologize for it."

She laughed, shaking her head. For a second, the stares didn't matter. The game was about to start, and we were ready to watch the Celtics take over.

As soon as the game tipped off, the row in front of us jumped to their feet, chanting "Defense!" loud enough to shake the rafters. I glanced at Alexis, expecting the same level of energy—but she was casually munching on popcorn like she was watching a rom-com instead of a high-stakes basketball game. She caught me looking and grinned, cheeks full.

"Want some?" she asked, holding out the bag like it was some kind of treasure.

I shook my head. "Nah, I'm good."

Still, for some reason, my mind drifted to Naomi. I had Alexis sitting right next to me, the game unfolding in front of us, but there she was—popping into my head like she had any business being there. It didn't make sense, especially not here, where the energy of the crowd kept pulling me back to the present.

By the second quarter, the arena erupted after a huge play, the sound rolling through the building like a wave. Every moment felt bigger than the last—wild cheers, frustrated groans, tension thick in the air with every close call. But by halftime, the scoreboard wasn't looking good for us. The Wizards were up 56-51, and the fans around us wasted no time letting us hear about it.

One guy turned to me with a smug grin. "Tough night for Celtics fans, huh?"

I frowned, leaning back like I wasn't worried. "There are always two halves to a game." I only half believed it, though. The way the Celtics were playing, we might be in for a rough night.

By the end of the third quarter, the Wizards clung to a one-point lead, and the game had turned into a nail-biter. Just when I thought the energy couldn't get any more intense, the entertainment break started—cheerleaders took the court, the mascot ran around stirring up the crowd, and then, right on cue, the Kiss Cam lit up the jumbotron.

Oh no. Not us. Please, not us.

I silently prayed, trying to act cool, but Alexis had other plans. She was bouncing in her seat, waving her arms like she actually wanted to be picked.

I looked up just in time to see the inevitable—our faces, front and center, plastered across the massive jumbotron for the entire arena to see.

Alexis' eyes widened before she burst out laughing. "Well, what are you waiting for, JB?" she teased, leaning in playfully.

The crowd cheered louder, egging us on. My face burned. My heart pounded. All I could think was, *God, please don't let me mess this up.*

"You better put one on the cheek before people start talking," Alexis hinted, tilting her head toward me with a grin.

The entire stadium seemed to be holding its breath, waiting. My palms were sweaty, my mind spinning. We weren't even a couple—just two friends at a game. But the crowd didn't care about that. They wanted a show.

What if I liked it? What if it was awkward?

I swallowed hard, then, before I could overthink it, licked my lips, closed my eyes like I was about to dive off a cliff, and planted a quick kiss on her cheek.

Relief washed over me. *That wasn't so bad.*

But apparently, the stadium disagreed.

A chorus of boos erupted around us, rolling through the crowd like a wave.

"That's not a real kiss!" a woman in front of us shouted, arms crossed like she was personally offended.

"Yeah, c'mon! You can do better!" another voice called from behind me.

I glanced at Alexis, who stood there shaking her head in mock disappointment, totally playing it up. I shrugged helplessly, feeling like I'd just missed a game-winning shot.

Then, before I could react, she grabbed my face and kissed me.

The crowd exploded.

Alexis kissed me hard, her lips warm and soft—and just for a second, she slipped in a little tongue. Buttered popcorn and mint. Weird combo, but not bad.

"That's more like it!" a husky, balding guy behind me bellowed, slapping me on the back so hard I nearly flew over the seat in front of me.

I straightened up, blinking at Alexis, who just winked and popped another piece of popcorn into her mouth like nothing had happened.

The cheers kept rolling through the arena, but all I could think about was the kiss. How could someone with such small lips be that good of a kisser? It didn't make sense, but suddenly, I wanted more.

I shook off the thought, forcing a smile and waving at a few lingering fans like I was some kind of celebrity. But for the next ten minutes, I sat there frozen, replaying that kiss in my head, over and over again.

"Are you okay?" Alexis leaned in, her voice soft as her hand rubbed slow circles on my back. She had to know I wasn't, but her eyes kept flicking between mine and my lips, like she was trying to read me.

"Yeah, I'm good. You just caught me off guard, that's all."

Lies. My heart pounded like I'd just sprinted a marathon. What was happening to me? I needed something stronger than soda, fast.

As the game carried on, I tried to lock back into it, but the thoughts wouldn't quit. My body finally started cooling down, but the intimacy of that kiss lingered, a fog I couldn't shake. I glanced at Alexis from the corner of my eye, my pulse still out of sync. Public displays of affection weren't my thing, but somehow, this felt different. It felt right. The ride home... that was going to be interesting.

With five seconds left in the game, the Celtics were down 96-90. I grabbed Alexis's hand, an instinctual move. "Let's get out of here before this crowd turns wild," I whispered, already planning our exit strategy.

"Good idea," Alexis said, weaving her fingers into mine as we made our way up the arena stairs. The crowd buzzed with post-game energy, thick and restless. We maneuvered through the masses, still laughing about the heat we caught for rocking Celtics gear in Wizards territory. It felt light, easy—until my eyes locked onto something.

Or rather, someone.

Fifteen feet ahead, holding hands with a short guy in a Yankees jacket and blue baseball cap, was Naomi.

I stopped walking. My feet felt like they were sinking, each step forward threatening to pull me into something I wasn't ready to face.

"I think that's Pastor Naomi," I muttered, my throat suddenly dry.

"Where?" Alexis scanned the crowd, then stopped cold when she spotted her. "That is her," she said, voice picking up speed.

Before I could stop her, she was pulling me toward them like a freight train. She let go of my hand, shot forward, and called out Naomi's name over the chaos of the crowd.

Naomi turned just as Alexis wrapped her in a hug, the two of them embracing like long-lost friends. And there I was, standing in the background, completely invisible, my heart pounding so hard it felt like it might burst out of my chest. Naomi hadn't seen me yet, and part of me wished it could stay that way.

"Hey, Alexis!" Naomi's voice was cheerful, unaware of the storm brewing in my head. They pulled back from the hug, Naomi smiling, still oblivious to my presence. "What are you doing here?"

The guy she was with shifted beside her, clearly not expecting this sudden interruption, but I could barely focus on him. My mind was stuck on one thing—getting out before I was seen. I took a step back, ready to slip into the crowd.

Then I heard it.

"JB? Is that you, man?"

I froze. That voice. No. Not now.

I turned on my heel, pasting on a fake smile. "Bryce."

He grinned wide, walking straight toward me. Before I could react, he pulled me into a brotherly hug, slapping my back like we were old friends. "What's up, man? What are you doing here?"

"Just came to catch the game," I managed, my mind scrambling. I needed to get out of here before everything imploded.

But Bryce wasn't done. "Bro, I'm so glad I ran into you! I've been wanting to introduce you to someone." He hooked his arm around my shoulder and started walking me toward Naomi.

My stomach twisted. "No, really, it's cool—"

Too late.

Naomi and Alexis were still chatting when Bryce interrupted, his voice booming. "Hey, honey! There's someone I want you to meet."

Honey?

He reached for Naomi's hand, gently pulling her toward us. My heart thundered as she turned, her expression shifting from lighthearted conversation to absolute shock. It was like slow motion, the way her eyes met mine.

All the color drained from her face. Her lips parted, but no words came out.

"JB, this is my wife, Naomi," Bryce said proudly, completely unaware to the emotional wreckage happening in real time. "Naomi, this is JB—the guy I was telling you about from the men's conference."

Wife.

The word slammed into me, knocking the air from my lungs. Naomi—the woman who had been constantly crossing my mind, showing up at my apartment, tangled up with me emotionally—was married. To Bryce.

Naomi tried to force a smile, but it was weak, and we both knew it. I was barely holding it together, but I managed to speak, though my voice felt hollow. "Oh... wow. Naomi. I didn't know..."

The sentence trailed off, unfinished, like everything between us.

Bryce tilted his head in confusion. "Wait... you two know each other?"

Naomi blinked rapidly, trying to regain composure. "Y-Yeah, JB and I know each other from church events," she said quickly, her voice tight, rehearsed.

"Yeah," I echoed, numb. "Church stuff."

Bryce beamed. "That's awesome! Small world, huh? We should all get together sometime, you know? Catch up properly."

I nearly choked. The last thing I wanted was to sit across from Bryce and Naomi, pretending everything was fine. But I forced a nod. "Yeah... maybe."

Naomi's eyes flicked between Alexis and me, filled with unspoken apologies and desperation. There was no fixing this.

Sensing the tension, Alexis, ever the social savior, chimed in. "Well, it was really nice seeing you both, but we should probably get going. You know, traffic getting out of here can be a nightmare."

"Yeah," I agreed quickly, seizing the out. "We should head out."

Bryce clapped me on the back again, flashing that big grin. "Alright, man! Let's stay in touch."

"Sure thing," I whispered, but all I wanted was to disappear.

As Alexis and I walked away, the noise of the arena returned in a rush, but all I could focus on was Naomi's face—the look that said everything we couldn't. I stole one last glance over my shoulder.

She was watching me leave, her eyes haunted and hollow, while Bryce chatted beside her, completely clueless.

Every step toward the exit felt heavier than the last. Alexis held my hand, talking about something, but I barely registered it.

My world had just shattered.

# CHAPTER 38

*Blessed is the pure in heart*

THE DRIVE HOME WAS SILENT. GOSPEL MUSIC PLAYED softly from my Spotify playlist, blending with the steady hum of the engine. A faint breeze slipped through the cracked window, carrying the scent of the Chick-fil-A nuggets I'd demolished earlier. As I merged onto I-95 toward Richmond,

I glanced over at Alexis. She stared out the window, her face calm, but something in her eyes told a different story. I hesitated before speaking. "You okay?" I asked, hoping to lighten the mood with a half-smile, though it felt more like a failed attempt.

She rested her hand on my arm, her touch warm. "I'm worried about you, JB. I'm here if you ever want to talk. No judgment, okay?"

I nodded, my chest tightening. "Thanks."

I wanted to believe Naomi had played me, that this was all on her. But deep down, I knew better. I'd ignored the signs, never asked the one question that could have saved me from this mess. *Are you married?* Maybe I didn't ask because I didn't want to know. Or maybe, deep down, I had set myself up to lose from the start.

"Hey, if you need to vent, I can be your therapist for the night," Alexis joked, nudging me lightly. "Only costs a hug and a bag of popcorn."

I let out a small chuckle, the tightness in my shoulders easing just a bit. "That's a pretty good deal. I'll take two hugs and a side of nachos."

"Done." She smiled. For a moment, the night didn't feel so heavy.

But the feeling didn't last. Reality crept back in, and I shook my head. "I just don't get it. How could Naomi do this? It feels like I was just a pawn in her game."

"Sometimes people have their own reasons," Alexis said gently. "But you're not a pawn, JB. You're the king of your own chessboard."

I smirked. "That's deep."

"Just trying to channel my inner philosopher," she grinned, tossing her hair over her shoulder.

The highway stretched ahead, endless, but somehow, the laughter we shared made it feel a little less lonely. Maybe I didn't have all the answers, but with Alexis by my side, I felt a little less lost.

Two hours later, I pulled into her driveway. The second I turned off the engine, I hopped out and walked over to open her door. When she stepped out, she wrapped her arms around my neck, holding me tight.

"Everything's going to be okay," she said softly, pressing a quick kiss to the side of my face. "God wants you to cast your cares on Him because He loves you."

Her perfume—something sweet and familiar—lingered in the cool night air. My gaze shifted to her lips. That kiss at the game flashed in my mind. For a split second, I wanted to kiss her again. But I couldn't. Not now. I wasn't about to mess this up by letting my emotions take over.

I took a step back. "Thanks for tonight."

She tilted her head, amusement dancing in her eyes. "What's on your mind?"

"Nothing."

Her smirk told me she wasn't buying it. "You're thinking about the kiss cam, aren't you?"

I raised an eyebrow. "And if I am?"

She crossed her arms. "I could tell you were uncomfortable."

"I was just being respectful! Didn't want to violate any public decency laws."

She burst out laughing. "Respectful? Please. That was the quickest, most awkward peck ever. You're lucky I took matters into my own hands."

I chuckled. "Guess I owe you a proper one next time."

"Oh, you better believe it." Her eyes sparkled with mischief.

I shook my head, grinning. "We may have lost the game, but at least we survived a stadium full of Wizards fans. I had a great time with you."

She held up her hand for a high five, which I gladly met.

"You're *Katt Williams* funny," I said, pulling her into another hug. "I hope we can do this again," I added.

"Absolutely." She leaned up and kissed the corner of my mouth, just enough to tease. "And JB? Never forget that God will never leave you nor forsake you. And neither will I."

As she unlocked her front door, she glanced back at me. "Text me when you get home, okay? I need my beauty sleep, but I also need to know you made it."

"You got it," I said, smiling.

"Goodnight, JB."

"Goodnight, Alexis."

I watched her disappear inside, then exhaled as I walked back to my truck. Something about tonight felt different. Maybe this was the start of something new.

But as I drove out of her subdivision, my thoughts circled back to Naomi. The look on her face tonight—troubled, almost guilty—stuck with me. How could she do this, knowing she was married? Why not just tell me the truth?

Then again, maybe honesty had never been part of the plan.

By the time I got home, it was past midnight. I leaned back against the headrest for a second, exhaling. Finally, I grabbed my phone and sent Alexis a quick text: Made it home.

Instead of heading straight to bed, I wandered into the kitchen. My mind wouldn't shut off. I needed something to take the edge off. My eyes landed on the bottle of scotch. I hesitated. I *should* pray. I *should* take this to God. But how could I? His word was clear. I'd messed up, and I knew it.

I sighed, grabbed a glass, and poured myself a drink. The ice clinked as I lifted it in a half-hearted toast. "Here's to me."

Just as I took a sip, my phone buzzed on the coffee table.

I frowned and picked it up.

A message from Naomi.

My chest tightened.

What could she possibly want?

# CHAPTER 39

*Bad women and unfaithful wives*

A MONTH HAD PASSED SINCE THAT NIGHT AT THE Wizards game, and I was at Gold's Gym, struggling through a set of fifty-pound curls. My arms burned, the weights felt heavier than usual, and no matter how hard I pushed, I couldn't shake the past month—couldn't outrun the memory of Naomi, Bryce, or the truth I never saw coming.

I told myself I was moving on. That it didn't matter anymore. Maybe even with Alexis.

At least, that's what I kept trying to convince myself.

I reached for my water bottle when my phone buzzed on the bench beside me. Unknown Caller.

Normally, I'd ignore it. But something—curiosity, instinct, maybe just plain stubbornness—had me swiping to answer.

"This is James," I said, peeling off my gloves as I slung my bag over my shoulder. I headed toward the treadmills, needing movement, something to ground me.

The voice on the other end stopped me cold.

"James?"

Soft. Unsteady. Familiar.

My pulse kicked up. "Yeah," I said, slower this time, stepping onto the treadmill. "Who's this?"

A pause. Then, barely above a whisper—

"It's me. *Naomi.*"

The name hit like a right hook. My thumb slammed the stop button on the treadmill before I even realized what I was doing. I stepped off, gripping my phone tighter, heartbeat pounding in my ears.

I barely registered the front desk guy's "Have a great day!" as I pushed open the glass doors, the cool air doing nothing to settle the heat rising in my chest.

"Why are you calling me?" I snapped, unlocking my truck. "And why from an unknown number?"

"I've been trying to reach you, James," she said, voice tight. "Every time I call from my number, it goes straight to voicemail. I've called over twenty times. Why haven't you answered?"

I let out a sharp, humorless laugh. "Take a wild guess."

Silence. Then, quieter, "I had to talk to you."

Frustration burned through me. "You think it's okay to tell another man you love him when you're married?" I shoved the key in the ignition. "It's not fair—to me, to your husband, and it's definitely not right with God."

A sharp breath came through the line, followed by silence. But I wasn't about to back down.

"Look, Naomi," I said, switching the call to Bluetooth as I backed out of the lot. "You're a good person. But this? It has to stop. Bryce is a good guy. He's done nothing wrong to me. I hope you have a great life with him."

I was ready to hang up, ready to be done with this for good—

But her voice cracked.

"It's not what you think," she said, and I hated how that pleading tone still got to me. "Please, James. Can we meet? Just to talk?"

My grip tightened on the steering wheel. "I can't."

"Is it Alexis? Are you seeing her now?"

"We've been hanging out," I said, knowing it was petty but wanting her to feel even an ounce of what she'd put me through.

The satisfaction barely lasted a second before guilt crept in, tightening in my chest. This wasn't me. I wasn't the type to play games, to throw things in someone's face just to get a reaction. But with Naomi, it was different.

Why did it even matter if I was talking to Alexis? Was I trying to prove something to her—or to myself? Maybe if I kept saying it, I'd start to believe Alexis was the one I wanted. That I was moving forward. Leaving all of this behind.

But Naomi had a way of pulling me back in, making me question everything.

She hesitated. "Alexis hasn't been to church since that night I saw you two at the game."

I frowned. "What?"

"I tried calling her too, but her phone goes straight to voicemail. Are you both avoiding me?"

"Maybe we're just done with this mess."

"Did you block me?" she asked, almost accusingly. "Because if you did, you wouldn't have seen the text I sent explaining everything."

I exhaled through my nose. "Yeah, I saw it. And I deleted it."

"You didn't even read it?"

or what? Closure's overrated—denial works just fine.

Neither of us spoke. Outside, the city lights streaked past, but my mind was stuck, circling the same thoughts.

I missed her. More than I wanted to admit.

But that didn't change the truth. She was married. And I wasn't about to make the same mistake twice.

James, please," she said, her voice unsteady. "Just meet me. One last time.

I knew what the right answer was. I knew what I should say. But still, I found myself asking—

"When and where?"

"Your house. In an hour."

The line went dead before I could respond.

I sat there, gripping the steering wheel, jaw clenched. Of course, she hung up before I could even agree. That was Naomi— always pulling the strings, always deciding how things played out. And here I was, still caught up in it.

What was I doing? Instead of letting it get to me, I pulled into a Jersey Mike's parking lot, rubbing my temples as a headache pressed behind my eyes. I needed food. And maybe divine intervention. Because whatever this was— It wasn't over yet.

What kind of game was she playing?

# CHAPTER 40

## Praying with selfish motives

I WASN'T SURE WHAT TO EXPECT WHEN NAOMI ARRIVED—more lies, more excuses. I knew I should walk away, but despite everything, I still wanted to see her.

I fell face-first onto my bed, wrestling with the urge to call the whole thing off. Why had I answered that call? I never picked up from unknown numbers. Was I getting soft?

Rolling onto my back, I stared at the ceiling fan, willing it to pull me away from this mess. The blades spun lazily above me, a blur of motion that only emphasized my stillness.

Did I really want to face her? A part of me longed for the comfort of her voice, the way she could light up a room with her laughter. Another part screamed at me to resist. *This isn't just about you anymore.*

I took a deep breath, trying to steady my racing heart. Whatever conversation lay ahead had the power to tip my life back into chaos. I'd fought too hard to break free from her web. But no matter how much I tried to ignore it, the pull was still there—undeniable, reckless, dangerous.

I closed my eyes and prayed.

**Dear God,**

**It's me again. I won't drag this out because You already know. I'm in sin. I'm entertaining a woman who isn't mine, and I don't know why I can't just say no. Forgive me. Help me walk the straight path. Let this conversation honor You. Keep me from falling back into the same trap.**

**In Jesus' name, Amen.**

The prayer should have made me feel better. Instead, guilt pressed down on me like a weight I couldn't shake. I let out a dry chuckle and sat up, running a hand over my face. Some Christian I am, huh?

Shaking my head at myself, I got up and made my way to the bathroom. Maybe a shower would help.

Ten minutes later, I stepped out, grabbed a towel, and dried off, feeling no better than before. At least now I was a clean mess.

Dressed and restless, I walked into the kitchen and grabbed a Corona from the fridge. Naomi would be here any minute, and the thought sent my stomach in knots. I sat at the kitchen bar, mentally rehearsing my lines like I was preparing for an audition. **How do you tell a married woman you don't want her drama anymore?**

Finishing my beer, I grabbed another and headed into the living room, where Acrimony played on the TV. A tale of betrayal and heartbreak—perfect. Just what I needed as a prelude to my own emotional train wreck.

A loud knock echoed through the apartment, making me jolt. Naomi wouldn't knock like that. It was the kind of knock that said, *Hurry up before someone sees me.*

I tiptoed to the door and peered through the peephole. Sure enough, there she was, glancing over her shoulder like she was expecting to be followed.

**Alright. Deep breath. You got this.**

I pulled the door open.

Unlike her usual entrances—bold, dramatic, unapologetic—this time, she stood there with her head down, like she was mourning a loss. When our eyes finally met, something in her gaze hit me deep. Fear. Sadness. Maybe even regret.

"Hey," she said softly.

"Hey," I replied, keeping my tone flat.

I stepped aside, and she walked straight to the living room, dropping onto the couch like she belonged there. She set her purse on the coffee table and locked eyes with me, searching for something unspoken.

The silence stretched thick between us, a game of who *will crack first.*

I finally stood up. "Want something to drink?" I asked, trying to sound detached, but we both knew I'd give in eventually.

She glanced at the beer in my hand. "I'll have what you're having."

I grabbed another bottle from the fridge and handed it to her.

She took a sip, set it down, and traced the rim with her finger before standing and walking toward me. I didn't move. My body tensed, caught between stepping back and pulling her closer.

"I'm sorry," she whispered. "I didn't want you to find out like that. It's not what you think. If you had read my text instead of blocking me, you'd know the truth."

"It's cool," I said, forcing indifference. But curiosity gnawed at me.

Her fingers brushed my jaw lightly. "The last time we were together, in your dining room, you told me you loved me," she murmured. "I need your heart, James. I need you."

I swallowed hard and stepped back. "But you're married."

She flinched.

"We can't do this. Ever."

I turned away, heading for the kitchen, needing space before I did something stupid. Naomi followed, settling onto the barstool beside me. "If you let me explain, everything will make sense," she pleaded.

I exhaled slowly, pressing my palms against the counter. "I'm listening."

Just as she was about to speak, my phone buzzed on the counter.

Alexis.

I snatched it up. "I have to take this." Without waiting for a response, I stepped into my bedroom and closed the door.

"Hello?"

"Hey, JB," Alexis's voice rang through, light and excited. "What are you up to?"

"Not much. What's up?"

"So, I scored two prime tickets to the *Chris Rock* show tonight. You in?"

Chris Rock? My favorite comedian? "Heck yes, I'm in!"

She laughed. "Awesome. But there's a catch… it's in Virginia Beach, and it starts at nine."

Two-hour drive? Didn't matter. "Can you be ready by 5:30?"

"Absolutely."

I hung up, grinning.

When I stepped back into the kitchen, Naomi stood by the counter, arms crossed. Her expression unreadable.

"Everything okay?" she asked.

"Yeah. Just a friend. Got an extra ticket to a comedy show."

She nodded, gaze dropping. "I just got a call from the church. I have to run out for a bit."

"Sure," I said, but I couldn't shake the feeling she was slipping away again.

I watched her leave, shutting the door on whatever tangled mess she always dragged in. But tonight, my mind wasn't on Naomi.

It was on Alexis.

The road trip.

The laughter ahead.

And for once, it felt like I was making the right choice.

# CHAPTER 41

## Hidden things will be exposed by God

AT 5:15 P.M., I GRABBED MY KEYS, AND HEADED TO MY truck, ready for an incredible night with Alexis. It had been years since I last saw Chris Rock live, and I couldn't wait. As I turned onto West Broad Street, old-school R&B blasted through the speakers, setting the perfect mood.

My Apple CarPlay lit up with an incoming call from Alexis. I glanced at the time—5:22. I was even early. For once, I was ahead of schedule. Smirking, I answered, ready to tease her about being on time.

But Alexis didn't give me the chance.

"Please forgive me, JB," she rushed out, "but Pastor Naomi just called an emergency meeting at the church tonight."

The words slammed into me, knocking the air from my lungs. "An emergency meeting?" I kept my voice steady, but my mind was already spinning.

"Yeah, she said it's something important that the church needs to hear. Everyone's on pins and needles."

*Pins and needles?* My gut clenched. It had to be about me. Naomi had to be planning to confess something, and if she did…

Was she going to mention my name?

The idea of her standing in front of the congregation, spilling everything, sent a spike of panic through me. My thoughts scrambled, leaping from one disaster to another. A thousand possibilities flashed through my mind, none of them good.

"What time is the meeting?" My voice cracked, betraying me.

"Five-thirty."

I snapped my eyes to the dashboard. 5:24 p.m.

There was no way I'd make it in time. I was at least thirty minutes away, and every second felt like sand slipping through my fingers. I slammed my foot on the gas, weaving through traffic like a man outrunning a storm.

"I'm on my way," I blurted before hanging up, gripping the wheel like it was the only thing keeping me grounded.

Of course. Of all days to be caught in a jam, today had to be the day. To my left, a car full of kids waved plastic guns at me, laughing like tiny little tyrants. I shot them a look and turned to my right—some couple blasting rock music so loud I felt like I was inside their speakers.

I smacked the steering wheel, a low curse slipping out. *This cannot be happening.* Every car in front of me felt like a roadblock. Every ticking second, another nail in the coffin of whatever disaster Naomi was about to unleash.

I wiped the sweat from my brow, muttering to myself. "Just keep moving, James. You have to get there."

But deep down, I wasn't sure I wanted to know what was waiting for me when I did.

By 6:00 p.m., the traffic finally inched forward, and minutes later, the road opened up. Relief washed over me as I pushed the speed limit, determined not to waste another second.

By 6:25 p.m., I screeched into the church parking lot—empty.

Not a single car in sight.

I was too late.

My stomach sank. What now? Had I just dodged a bullet, or had I walked straight into an ambush without even knowing it?

I yanked out my phone and called Alexis. The call rang once before going straight to voicemail. My pulse quickened, anxiety creeping up my spine.

*Had Naomi told the entire church about us?*

But then again—had we really sinned? There hadn't been a kiss. A touch. Nothing that crossed the line. But it still felt like we had played with fire.

I needed answers.

And that meant talking to the last person I wanted to call— *Bryce.*

I gritted at the thought of him. If things had gone down, he'd know. And I had no doubt he'd be waiting for the chance to throw it in my face.

I scrolled to his number and hit dial.

"The number you are trying to reach is not in service."

Typical.

This whole thing was spiraling out of control, and the one person who could clear it up was conveniently unreachable.

Which left me with one option.

*Naomi.*

My finger hovered over her name, hesitation creeping in. Calling her meant crossing a line. If she answered, every buried truth, every lie we told ourselves—it could all come crashing down. But if she didn't, I'd be left in the dark, suffocating on my own worst fears.

I took a deep breath, unblocked her number, and hit dial.

The phone rang once.

Twice.

Each second stretched, stirring up every doubt I'd been trying to bury.

Just as I was about to hang up, she answered.

"James?" Her voice was soft, uncertain.

Hearing her say my name made in that tone couldn't be good.

"Naomi," I forced the word out. "I need to know... what happened at the meeting?"

Silence.

Not static. Not background noise. Just her, breathing—deliberate, measured, like she was piecing together something that would change everything.

Then, finally, she spoke. "James... it's done."

A knot formed in my chest. "What's done?"

The pause that followed was long enough to make my grip tighten around the phone.

Then, in a voice so quiet I almost missed it—

"Everything."

# CHAPTER 42



**"MY SECRET'S OUT."**

Naomi's voice was calm, almost soothing—except it had the exact opposite effect on me.

"What secret?" My voice came out too high-pitched, like a teenager caught sneaking in past curfew.

She paused. A long, unbearable pause. Then she laughed.

This wasn't funny. This was my life. My reputation. My standing in the church. Alexis.

And she was laughing.

"I'm waiting," I snapped, harsher than I meant to.

"Are you sure your ego can handle it?" she teased, her smirk practically coming through the phone. "Men are so fragile. One little crack and—poof."

I exhaled hard, pressing my fingers to my temple. She was playing games, and I wasn't in the mood. And why was I sweating?

"Enough. Just tell me."

I pulled into my apartment complex, barely remembering the drive. My hands were sweaty on the wheel, my heart pounding so hard I could hear it. I parked, bolted up the stairs, and went straight for the Dom Pérignon in the cabinet. Popped the top. Took a long swig.

Naomi's voice was steady. "I'm pregnant, James."

The bottle froze at my lips.

The kitchen light buzzed. The fridge rattled. The city noise outside carried on. But my brain? It stopped working.

*No. No way.*

I took another drink, the alcohol burning its way down, but it didn't help. Nothing could cut through the roaring in my head.

"What do you mean… *pregnant?*"

For half a second, I felt relieved. At least I wasn't the church scandal. Yet.

But that relief disappeared just as fast. Something colder took its place.

I pressed a hand over my face. "How?" Dumb question. I already knew how.

The answer clicked into place. **Bryce.** It had to be Bryce.

"I bet he's excited," I said, though I wasn't happy. How could Naomi lead me on like this knowing she was pregnant by Bryce. At once, I wanted to end the call but the next thing she said shook me to the core.

"Bryce isn't the father."

The phone almost slipped from my hand.

"You are."

I dropped it.

A dull thud. The sound of my last shred of sanity hitting the floor.

I grabbed the bottle again and took another long sip, trying to drown out the kind of panic that makes you question every life choice that led to this moment..

This had to be a nightmare.

I snatched the phone back up, my fingers clumsy. "What in the mother of Jesus are you talking about?" My voice cracked. "We've never—Naomi, we've never even—" I ran a hand over my face, my breathing all over the place. "There's no way. You're lying."

Her voice stayed maddeningly calm. "I'm having a baby by the Holy Spirit. And you, James… you are the father."

My brain short-circuited.

I needed *Maury Povich* to appear from behind my couch, waving a DNA test.

My mouth opened, but nothing came out. My pulse was racing, my thoughts tripping over themselves.

"You're telling me I'm some kind of modern-day Joseph?" My laugh came out weird and broken.

"Haven't you heard of the Virgin Mary?" she said, dead serious.

I stared at the champagne in my hand. Was I drunk? Had I downed the whole bottle? My vision blurred for a second.

And then—Naomi burst out laughing.

I exhaled sharply, my whole body sagging into the couch. "You're joking."

"Relax," she said, still laughing. "I'm not pregnant. The news is about my dad retiring. I'm taking over the church."

I let my head fall back against the couch, staring at the ceiling. Silence.

Then—"You're not pregnant?" I needed to hear it again, just to be sure.

"Nope."

Another beat of silence. Then, casually—

"But I am on my way to your place. We need to finish this conversation. See you in an hour."

The line went dead.

I let the phone slide out of my hand and took one last sip of champagne.

I really need to stop dialing her number like it won't cost me every ounce of peace I have left.

# CHAPTER 43

## Controlled by the Spirit or the flesh

POPPING A FEW ALTOIDS, I LEANED AGAINST THE WINDOW-sill, staring out like a dog waiting for its owner. It was ridiculous—pathetic even. But I couldn't help it.

Naomi's joke still rattled in my head—pregnant by the Holy Spirit. Straight out of the Bible. And the worst part? I almost fell for it. Joseph had an angel to set the record straight—me? I'd need a notarized letter from heaven. Preferably with a signature.

Funny how close I came to losing my mind over something so impossible.

Instead of staring out the window like some kind of peeping Tom, I made my way to the kitchen, trying to ignore the fact that my stomach was waging a full-blown war. The "feed me now or regret it" battle had begun, and my stomach was definitely winning. The fridge held nothing new—just the same sad leftovers. I grabbed a few slices of pizza, tossed them in the oven, and sank into a chair. Scrolling through Candy Crush, I swiped absently, trying to trick my mind into calm.

Ten minutes later, with steaming pizza and a bottle of water, I crashed onto the couch and hit play on *Acrimony*—again. *Taraji P. Henson* was electric, downright terrifying, like she had the devil on speed dial. No way she shouldn't have won an Oscar. I knew every scene, every twist, but still, I couldn't look away.

Then came the knock. Soft, but enough to slice through the rare quiet. My breath hitched—nerves and something else I didn't care to name.

I checked the peephole—there she was, grinning like she'd just won the lottery.

I cracked the door open, but before I could say a word, she breezed past me, straight to the living room—like Black Friday, and I was standing between her and a 70% off sale. She grabbed a slice of pizza and took a massive bite.

"This is good," she said through a full mouth. "You didn't want this, did you?"

I exhaled, half in disbelief. "Go for it."

She settled in without hesitation, devouring the pizza like she'd been starving for days. For someone so petite, she ate with the enthusiasm of a linebacker at an all-you-can-eat buffet.

"You sure you don't want any?" she teased, reaching for another slice and popping the cap off my water like she owned it. After a long gulp, she wiped her mouth with the back of her hand, then locked eyes with me. "So... you're not ready to be a father, huh?"

The way she said it—half-joking, half-digging—unsettled me. I shifted, debating whether to laugh it off or take the bait. Instead, I stood and headed to the kitchen, my appetite for pizza officially gone.

"Want something stronger to drink?" I called, still amused by how easily she took over my space. At this point, I should probably just give her a key.

"I'll have whatever you're having."

Before I could respond, she was already beside me, rummaging through the cupboard like she owned the place. She pulled out a bag of chili-flavored Doritos, tearing it open like a pro.

"And why are you watching that crazy movie again?"

I smirked, grabbing two glasses. "Oh, so now we're about to debate *Acrimony*?"

"I'm just saying—you do know it was the guy's fault she lost her mind, right?"

I laughed, shaking my head as I pulled out a half-empty bottle of Dom Pérignon. "And why is it always the man's fault?"

She grinned, clutching the Doritos like I'd tried to steal her last meal. Then, with that effortless confidence that made people look twice, she sauntered into the living room. I followed, setting her glass down in front of her.

"Because," she said, popping another chip in her mouth, "it usually is."

I took a sip of champagne, still burning with curiosity about what went down at church.

"So," I leaned forward, "tell me what happened at church. And don't leave out any details."

Kicking off her pink and white Nikes, she stretched out on the couch like she owned the place, arms behind her head as if she were settling in for a long therapy session.

She rolled onto her side, letting out an exaggerated yawn.

"Well…" she started, but before she could say another word, her eyes fluttered shut.

I waited. Maybe she was just thinking. But after a few seconds, her breathing evened out, and I realized—she was out. Just like that.

I shook my head, amused.

Only Naomi could show up unannounced, hijack my pizza, stir up my emotions, and then fall asleep like she had nothing better to do.

For a moment, I just watched her. Her face, usually so full of sharp remarks and mischief, was completely relaxed. Peaceful, even. It was rare to see her this still.

I debated waking her up—maybe nudging her and making her go home. But something about the way she curled up, like she belonged there, made me hesitate.

Instead, I grabbed a blanket from the linen closet and draped it over her.

Shaking my head, I headed to my room.

I must've dozed off for all of ten minutes when I caught the faint scent of Naomi's perfume—sweet, warm, and close.

Too close.

I blinked, groggy. Then I realized—she was curled up next to me, her arm draped across my chest like we were more than just friends.

*This was not good.*

# CHAPTER 44

*God will give you a way out of temptation*

HOW DID SHE EVEN GET IN HERE WITHOUT ME KNOWING?

I'm a light sleeper, always alert—the kind of person who wakes up at the sound of a pin dropping, a door shifting, even a breeze slipping through a cracked window. But somehow, Naomi had moved through my room like a shadow, and now here she was, draped across me like we were anything more than complicated friends.

Was I that comfortable around her? Comfortable enough to let my guard down completely?

And why did she have to smell like vanilla and strawberries, like temptation wrapped in sweetness?

I needed to pray.

**God,**

**Did You do this? Is this some kind of test? Because the last time I checked, she was out cold on the couch. But now—now she's here, sprawled across my bed like an invitation I didn't ask for.**

**Wait—no. That's not right. You would never tempt me with sin. I'm sorry. That was out of line.**

**But... look at her. Just look at her.**

**She's beautiful, God, and it's messing with me.**

I squeezed my eyes shut, breathing slow, steady, trying to find my footing in the storm brewing inside me.

**I don't want to give in to temptation. I want to serve You, to be obedient. But this—this is hard. Give me strength, because right now? I'm not feeling very strong.**

I opened my eyes, staring up at the ceiling like it held the answers I was praying for.

**Help me get through this without making a mess of everything.**

My heartbeat pounded in my ears as I inched toward the edge of the bed, every nerve on high alert. Just as I thought I might make it, Naomi moved, her arm slipping from my chest like she could feel the distance. Then—her eyes fluttered open.

She locked onto me, soft and drowsy. "Don't go," she said, yawning as she tugged me back toward the middle of the bed with surprising strength.

Before I could react, we were face-to-face, her lips inches from mine, her breath a mix of champagne and pepperoni. I should have been disgusted, but somehow, it was intoxicating.

Her arms slid around my neck, pulling me closer. My mind screamed no, but my body—my traitorous body—was ready to betray me. Just as our lips were about to meet, I turned my head slightly. Her mouth brushed the side of my face instead.

*That was too close. Way too close.*

The warmth of her skin, the way she fit against me—it was too much. The tension crackled like a live wire, sparking, dangerous, inevitable. I could feel myself slipping.

I shot upright and bolted from the bed, making a beeline for the bathroom. The door slammed shut behind me, and I twisted the lock, bracing myself against the sink like it was the only thing keeping me from falling apart.

In the mirror, my reflection stared back at me—wide-eyed, breathing hard, fighting a battle I wasn't sure I could win.

I *wanted* her.

God, I wanted her more than anything.

But this wasn't right.

My whole body ached with the pull of wanting her close, but the pit in my stomach told me everything I needed to know. If I gave in, there was no coming back from it.

I cranked on the faucet, splashing cold water onto my face, trying to shake the heat burning through me. *Be strong.* The words looped in my head, but part of me resented them. I didn't want to be strong. I wanted the easy way—the sweet surrender of falling into temptation.

I gripped the sink tighter, jaw clenched.

This was a battleground. And my soul was fighting for its life.

I took a breath. Another.

When I finally felt steady enough to face the world again, I unlocked the door, wincing at the loud creak as I peeked out.

Naomi was curled up in the middle of the bed, fast asleep, hugging a pillow to her chest.

*Lucky pillow.*

I exhaled and tiptoed into the living room.

The remote sat on the coffee table. I grabbed it, flipping on the TV, letting the familiar chaos of *Acrimony* fill the silence. Anything to drown out the war raging inside me.

A half-full glass of champagne still rested on the table. Without thinking, I picked it up and downed what was left.

I sank deeper into the couch, eyes glued to the screen, but my mind wasn't on the movie. Every twist, every betrayal, every scene—it all felt too familiar. Like I was living it, not watching it.

Eventually, exhaustion won. My eyes grew heavy, and before I knew it, sleep took me under.

When I woke up, the blanket I'd draped over Naomi was covering me.

My stomach tightened as I rubbed the sleep from my eyes, scanning the room. That's when I noticed it—a folded note on pink paper, sitting on the coffee table.

I leaned in, catching the faint trace of her perfume.

I didn't want to wake you. You looked so peaceful (and handsome). When you wake up, call me. I ran out to grab dinner. I hope you don't mind—I took your keys.

Guess you're stuck with me for the night.

See you soon.

—Naomi

I swallowed hard, gripping the note like it held some kind of answer.

*Stuck with her for the night.*

This just got a whole lot more complicated.

# CHAPTER 45

*Test every spirit*

MY MIND RACED. WHAT DID SHE MEAN SHE TOOK MY keys? And while I was sound asleep at that! The implications hit me all at once, like a storm rolling in fast.

*What if she made copies?* Naomi could have full access to my apartment—my truck, though? Probably not. That was secure, part of the programming. But what about my storage unit? My mailbox? The security deposit box stashed away in my closet, filled with every crucial document I owned? Just thinking about it sent a chill through me.

I snatched my phone off the coffee table and dialed her number. Straight to voicemail. No ringing, no nothing.

*Calm down.* I forced a breath, pushing back the panic. Instead of spiraling, I grabbed my spare truck key and bolted outside.

The last thing I wanted was to involve the police—on a pastor, no less—for stealing my vehicle.

But there it was, parked exactly where I left it. Relief swept through me, but it was short-lived.

Back inside, my phone buzzed. A missed call from Naomi. Then a text.

I'll be there in five minutes.

Before I could process that, another message flashed across my screen.

*Alexis.*

My chest tightened. *Alexis? Now?* It felt like the universe was setting me up for something, and I wasn't sure I was ready for it.

Hey JB,

I wanted to reach out and apologize for canceling our plans at the last minute. There's been a big change in church leadership, and Naomi is being installed as the new senior pastor this Sunday. I know it's a lot to take in, and I'm really sorry for the sudden change.

I promise I'll make it up to you! Hope you're having a great day despite everything. Call me later if you can.

So Naomi was telling the truth after all.

I exhaled, folding up the blanket and tossing it back into the linen closet. This was too much to process all at once. And just as I was piecing it together, I heard the unmistakable sound of a key turning in my front door.

"Honey, I'm home."

Naomi's voice rang out, full of playfulness, followed by her signature chuckle.

I turned, and there she was, standing in my doorway with a large paper bag stamped *Maggiano's Little Italy* in bold letters. That was in Short Pump, the upscale part of Richmond—known for incredible Italian food. I hadn't been there in years, but after watching her devour my pizza earlier, I was more than ready for this.

"I hope you like chicken parmesan and spaghetti," she grinned, stepping inside like she'd been living here for years.

"That sounds perfect."

Her energy was infectious, but my mind was still tangled in everything that had happened—or hadn't happened—in the last few hours. The text from Alexis. The church gossip. Naomi's sudden rise in power. And now here she was, moving through my space like we were playing house.

I set the bag on the counter, glancing at her. "So you weren't lying about the leadership change at church, huh?"

She smirked, unpacking the food. "I told you I wasn't. You should believe me more often, James. I'm not as complicated as you think."

I let out a laugh. Naomi? Simple? That was like calling a tornado a breeze.

I watched her plate up the food, her fingers grazing the sauce as she licked them clean. But there was no way she'd forgotten about slipping into my bed last night. No way that was just sleepwalking. And then there was Bryce. That night at the Wizards game still lingered like a bad aftertaste. I could still picture the way she laughed at his jokes, the way she lit up around him, while I sat on the sidelines, feeling like an outsider in my own life.

I needed answers.

"Naomi," I started, careful to sound casual. "About the other night… and, well, this morning." I met her gaze. "You, uh, slipped into my bed while I was asleep. That wasn't exactly nothing."

She didn't flinch as she set down the last plate, but the air in the room shifted.

The wine had completely worn off, and I was in my right state of mind. It's funny how alcohol tricks you into thinking you've got the courage of a lion, but when it fades, you're left staring at the aftermath. Things said, actions taken—things sober you would've thought twice about.

Maybe I should quit drinking altogether.

My eyes drifted to the wine cabinet. Thirty bottles lined up like trophies. Maybe I'd stop after finishing those.

Dinner was hearty, and *The Best Man Holiday* left us both in a relaxed mood, but the words I needed to say sat heavy on my tongue.

I cleared my throat. "Naomi, there's a lot we haven't talked about. I think it's time we do."

She raised an eyebrow, swirling the last sip of champagne in her glass. "Bryce? What about him?"

I leaned against the counter, arms crossed. "The night at the Wizards game... you two seemed—well, close. And then you told me I was the father of your Holy Spirit baby. What's the deal?"

Her smile flickered, just for a second. She took a slow sip of champagne, as if weighing her words. "Bryce and I... it's complicated." She sighed. "We've been through a lot. But what you saw that night—it's not what you think."

"Not what I think?" I stepped closer. "You were acting like a married couple, Naomi."

"We were married, James. Past tense. Our relationship ended long before that game. But... sometimes things blur, especially when you've shared so much history." She sighed, placing the glass down. "Bryce is part of my past, but I'm trying to move forward."

Her honesty disarmed me, but something still felt off. "And what about us? What are we, then?"

She looked up at me, her eyes soft but serious. "I guess that's what we need to figure out, isn't it?"

I didn't hesitate. I pulled her in and kissed her, pouring every ounce of emotion into it. Her lips were soft, warm, familiar. And just like that first night I saw her at church, the spark roared back to life.

She didn't pull away. She kissed me back, her hands gripping my arms as our bodies molded together. Without breaking the kiss, I scooped her up in my arms and—

"James? James, wake up."

My eyes shot open.

I was curled up on the couch, the blanket still draped over me. Wiping the drool from my mouth, I blinked up at Naomi. She stood over me, grinning, a white plastic bag labeled *Mama J's* in her hand.

"What?" I sat up, heart slamming against my ribcage.

She laughed. "I don't know, but that must've been some dream." She turned toward the kitchen, her laughter trailing behind her.

*Dream? That was a dream?*

I ran a hand down my face, my brain struggling to catch up. It had felt so real. The food, the conversation, the kiss. The way her lips—

I patted my pocket, suddenly panicked. My keys were there. Right where they should be.

My phone.

I snatched it up and scrolled. No message from Alexis. Nothing about the church.

I stared at the screen, my stomach twisting.

Had any of it happened? Or was I still dreaming?

# CHAPTER 46



NO WAY. I WIPED THE SWEAT FROM MY BROW. THAT couldn't have been a dream. It was too real—too vivid. Every detail was seared into my memory like a brand.

I glanced out the window, heart hammering. My truck was parked right in front—not twenty yards away like I'd imagined. My pulse quickened. If it really happened, then the Maggiano's bag had to still be in the kitchen.

I tore through the trash. Nothing.

My gaze landed on the glass of champagne still sitting on the table, half-full, untouched. A contradiction.

A sinking feeling clawed at my gut as I hurried into my bedroom, searching for any trace of Naomi—a dent in the pillows, the scent of her perfume. But the sheets were smooth, untouched, carrying only the fresh scent of detergent.

I stood in the middle of the room, my breath shallow. None of it made sense.

That was it—no more drinking. I needed a clear head, but instead, I felt like I was stuck between two realities, unsure which one was real.

**Unless—**

Maybe Naomi was messing with me. A cruel joke. *The moment we shared—was it real?*

Forcing myself to stay cool, I strolled into the kitchen and perched on a barstool, masking the unease creeping up my spine. "So, you don't remember anything about what we did just a few minutes ago?" I rubbed my temples, watching her closely.

Naomi shot me a look like I had three heads. "Seriously, James. You really need to stop drinking."

"No way," I muttered. "That was a dream?"

She arched an eyebrow, amusement flickering in her eyes. "I got you two pieces of catfish, macaroni and cheese, and collard greens. And for dessert, a slice of German chocolate cake." She smirked. "Hope it's as good as that dream of yours?"

She laughed—light, easy. It should have put me at ease, but instead, it tangled my thoughts even more.

Still dazed, I shook my head. "So you really don't remember?"

Naomi leaned against the counter, smirking. "James, you're too young to be a dementia candidate." A fleeting smile softened her face before she grabbed our plates and headed to the living room.

"Let's just eat and watch a movie. The Passion of the Christ is on."

I hesitated, then followed, my mind still stuck in the dream—or whatever it was.

"Don't forget napkins and drinks!" she called.

I managed a chuckle. "Fiji water for you, lemonade for me."

Naomi blinked, surprised. "No champagne?"

"No," I said firmly, still trying to shake the remnants of my earlier buzz. "I want to enjoy my meal without feeling inebriated."

She laughed, scooping up a forkful of mac and cheese. "Didn't have you pegged as the type to overdo it."

I barely heard her. My focus was locked on her, the ghost of that kiss still lingering in my mind. It had felt real, electric—like something I wasn't meant to wake up from.

If it was just a dream, why did it feel like I'd lost something?

As dinner settled in my stomach, a yawn slipped out before I could stop it.

"Sounds like somebody needs a nap," Naomi teased. "I still can't believe you inhaled both pieces of that monster fish like it was a Skittle. Your grocery bill must be insane."

I stretched out on the couch, sinking into the cushions. "Well, I'm 230 pounds with less than ten percent body fat. I like to eat. Guess that makes me a foodie."

But even as I said it, I knew I wasn't just talking about food.

I was consuming something else—something deeper, something I wasn't ready to name.

The more I tried to push it down, the more it clawed its way back up.

Would I ever uncover the truth, or was I just circling the same question, lying to myself about what—or *who*—I truly wanted?

*Naomi* or *Alexis?*

# CHAPTER 47



I WAS UP BRIGHT AND EARLY, ALREADY DREADING THE three-hour flight to Chicago. An all-day conference awaited me, where I was slated as a guest speakers for a Fortune 500 company. My task? Motivating a room full of high-paid attorneys who apparently needed a push to reignite their careers.

I scoffed at the thought—so making over $250K a year wasn't enough of a spark? What more did they need? A personal cheerleader?

Yawning,I rubbed the sleep from my eyes and stretched on the couch where I'd crash for the night. Naomi had taken my bed, a decision I'd made to be a gentleman—though the thought of her sleeping in my room had lingered all night.

As I sat up, something on the coffee table caught my eye. A handwritten note with *James* penciled across the front.

I hesitated, blinking hard. *Please, let this not be another dream.*

Slowly, I picked it up and unfolded it.

Dear James,

I hope this note finds you well-rested and feeling the goodness of the Lord. I decided to sneak out early so you could get the rest you need before your trip. I know you're going to energize the crowd today - I even read your speech last night and made a few comments. Lol.

Call me when you get to the airport so I can wish you a safe flight. Thank you for giving up your bed—it made me feel at home. And, confession: I miss you already. I hope you're okay with me being honest about how I feel. You're a wonderful man, James, and I'm looking forward to hanging out when you get back.

Have a blessed day!

Naomi

P.S. I left something for you. It's under your pillow.

I read it twice, my heart thudding in my chest. Her words felt so genuine, so unguarded. *She even went through my speech?*

I smiled. But then my eyes landed on the last line.

*I left something for you under your pillow.*

Curiosity overtook me. *A dream? A test? A challenge?*

Rising from the couch like an old man, I strolled into my bedroom, dragging my feet but secretly excited, like a kid on Halloween anticipating a bag full of candy.

Rising from the couch, I stretched like an old man, then strolled into my bedroom, dragging my feet but secretly excited—like a kid on Halloween, anticipating a bag full of candy.

The room surprised me. Naomi had made the bed, changed the linens, even opened the blinds. The morning sun poured in, flooding the space with warmth. Nice touch.

I reached under the pillow, fingers brushing against something cool and metallic.

A silver rope chain. Dangling from it—a small silver key.

I turned it over in my palm, examining it. Then, without thinking, I fastened the clasp around my neck. It sat perfectly—not too long, not too short. But a *key*?

What was she trying to tell me?

A grin tugged at my lips. No one had ever given me jewelry before. The only thing I owned that even resembled jewelry was my Apple Watch. This felt… *personal. Significant.*

Before I could overthink it, I grabbed my phone to text her—only to see she had beaten me to it.

Naomi:

You can thank me for the gift when you land safely in Chicago. Then, I'll tell you what the key means. Now stop stalling and get yourself ready to catch your flight.

I chuckled. She knew me too well—always one step ahead.

Stripping off my clothes, I stepped into the shower, letting the warm water wash away my grogginess—but not my thoughts. The key. *What did it unlock?* A secret? A memory? A piece of Naomi's past?

The question gnawed at me, but I pushed it aside. For now, I had to focus on my flight.

An hour later, freshly packed and with my rollaway suitcase in hand, I slid into my truck and made it to the airport in record time.

After retrieving my boarding pass, I breezed through security—TSA was surprisingly quick today. At Gate B12, I spotted a seat away from the growing crowd. Perfect.

Sinking into it, I pulled out my phone, ready to kill time with a quick game of chess.

That's when I saw her.

A well-dressed woman with striking platinum-colored hair, striding toward me with a confident smile.

*Uh oh.*

She stopped beside me. "Is this seat taken?"

I glanced around. Plenty of other open seats, yet she had picked the one right next to me.

With an exaggerated sigh, I realized there was no graceful way out of this.

"Yeah, nobody's sitting there," I muttered.

She slid into the seat, nudging my arm off the armrest in the process. Seriously?

Without a word, she pulled a sleek Apple laptop from her bag and got to work, typing away with swift, deliberate strokes.

I exhaled, shifting slightly. She was so close she might as well have been sitting in my lap.

I focused on my phone, pretending to be lost in my game. Maybe if I looked busy enough, she'd take the hint.

*No such luck.*

"So, you're heading to Chicago?" she asked, far too friendly for my liking.

"Yep." I didn't look up.

"I'm heading there too."

Great. My bubble of privacy had officially popped.

With a sigh, I caved. "Business or pleasure?"

She smirked. "Business is always a pleasure, and pleasure is always business."

*Oh, she's one of those.*

She leaned in slightly, lowering her voice like we were sharing a secret. "I'm speaking at an event. Motivating a room full of attorneys who've lost their spark."

I froze.

No way.

I turned toward her, *really* looking at her this time. "You're kidding."

Her eyes twinkled. "Why? You a lawyer in need of motivation?"

I smirked. "No, but I *am* speaking at that same event."

She blinked, then let out a low, amused laugh. "Well, well. Small world."

I shook my head. *Too small.*

My initial reluctance melted into curiosity. "What's your talk called?"

She tilted her head, her smile playful. "'Living the Life You've Always Wanted, No Matter Who Agrees.'"

I arched a brow. "Sounds… inspiring."

"You should stop by," she said, standing and extending a hand. "Barbara Gun."

I shook it. "James Barnes. Pleasure, Barbara."

"The pleasure's all mine."

By the time the boarding announcement echoed through the terminal, we had exchanged contact info.

Finally settling into my first-class seat, I reached into my bag, pulled out my Dre Beats headphones, and activated noise cancellation.

I picked my *slow jams* playlist, closed my eyes, and let the music drown everything out.

The stress of the morning faded.

Naomi. The *key*. The stranger I now knew as Barbara Gun.

For now, I let it all slip away.

And before I knew it, I was out.

# CHAPTER 48

*God or the enemy: who will you follow?*

THE TWO-DAY CONFERENCE HAD FINALLY WRAPPED up, and I couldn't have been more relieved. I'd checked out of my hotel early, grabbed an Uber straight to the airport, and now all I wanted was to be home. Traveling might have seemed glamorous to some, but after more than fifty trips a year, it was starting to feel like a grind.

I had a direct flight to Richmond, and the thought of a hot shower and my own bed was the only thing keeping me upright. The plane landed a little after 9 PM, and as I stepped off, I made sure to keep my headphones on and my facemask pulled low. The last thing I needed was small talk. People always seemed to pick the worst times to strike up a conversation, and tonight, I just wasn't in the mood.

As I strolled through the terminal toward the parking garage, I shot a quick text to Naomi to let her know I'd landed safely, just as I'd promised.

> **Me:** I made it back to Richmond safely. Should be home by 10. Just checking in, as you instructed Lol. Call whenever. Peace.

Even as I hit send, my mind kept circling back to the silver key she'd left for me. What was it for? What was the significance behind it? Keys usually opened doors, revealed something hidden, or granted access to something valuable. But this one? It seemed to unlock more questions than answers.

By the time I pulled into my apartment complex, exhaustion clung to me like a second skin. Dragging myself upstairs, I dropped my suitcase by the washer and stripped off my clothes, tossing everything straight into the machine. The sooner I could wash off the stench of the airport, the better. Just as I was about to step into the shower, my phone buzzed.

Barbara.

> **Barbara:** It was great to meet you, James. I hope you made it home safely. I'll be in Peoria visiting friends for a few days, but next week, I'll be in your area. Maybe we can catch up for a drink? My treat. Didn't want much, just saying hi. Oh, and here's a pic of me, in case you forgot what I look like.

I barely finished reading before my jaw dropped. Attached was a picture of her in a bold, red two-piece swimsuit that left little to the imagination. Her body was sculpted, toned in a way that made it impossible not to stare. The kind of effortless perfection that looked like it belonged on the cover of a fitness magazine.

I exhaled sharply, dragging a hand down my face. My thoughts drifted somewhere they shouldn't, but before they could wander too far, my phone rang.

*Naomi.*

Perfect timing.

"Hey there," she chirped before I could even say hello.

I sighed, already knowing this wasn't going to be a short conversation. Turning off the shower, I grabbed my robe from the back of the door and slumped onto the edge of the bed. My body felt like it weighed a ton.

"Hey," I muttered, my voice dragging with fatigue.

"So, tell me all about your trip! Did you inspire everyone like I know you did? And don't leave out any details." She was full of energy, and I could barely keep my head up.

"It was good," I said. "A bunch of well-off attorneys just try- ing to 'get their groove back,' like Stella." I chuckled weakly as I shuffled back to the bathroom and turned the shower on again.

"But can I call you after I clean up real quick? I feel like I've got the whole airport still on me."

I prayed she'd take the hint. But instead, she threw me a curveball.

"Are you hungry?"

I glanced at the clock on my nightstand. 10:23 p.m. I was starving, but exhaustion had the upper hand. "I am, but I'll probably just make a sandwich or something after I shower. Why?"

A pause. A beat longer than usual.

"I'm *outside* your apartment, silly. I made you a plate of food. Figured you'd be hungry, so I decided to stop by. Open the door. I'll be up in a minute."

I stared at my phone, my stomach twisting. *Please tell me I'm dreaming,* I thought, tilting my head toward the ceiling as if the heavens might offer me some kind of reprieve. But no divine intervention was coming. I sighed, shuffling to the door.

The lock clicked—a surrender. Whatever happened to being invited over first? Clearly, Naomi played by different rules.

As I swung the door open, the tie on my robe snagged on the doorknob. In a split second, my robe flew open—panic shot through me like a lightning bolt. I yanked it shut just in time, heart pounding, before Naomi even had a chance to look.

Bullet dodged.

She strolled in, oblivious to my near disaster. "You look comfortable," she teased, holding up the plate of food. "I figured you could use a home-cooked meal after all that traveling."

I tried to play it cool, even as my pulse struggled to settle. "You have no idea. Thank you. This looks great, but I really need to shower first. Give me a minute, and I'll be right back."

"Take your time," she said, already making herself at home in the living room.

Grateful for the extra time to compose myself, I stepped into the shower, hoping to scrub away the exhaustion. But once the hot water hit me, I realized just how wiped out I was. A few minutes stretched longer than they should have, and before I knew it, I was back in my room, towel-drying my hair.

I just needed to rest my eyes for a second.

Thirty minutes later, Naomi hadn't heard a word from me. Growing impatient, she walked down the hall, pushed open my bedroom door, and found me sprawled across the bed, out for the count.

She stood in the doorway, shaking her head. "Of course."

# CHAPTER 49

*Divine revelation*

THE NEXT MORNING, I WOKE TO THE UNMISTAKABLE smell of sizzling bacon and the blaring sounds of gospel music echoing from the kitchen. My head throbbed slightly, last night feeling like a distant haze. Blinking against the morning light, I stretched out, the cool sheets grounding me. Then I glanced down at myself and smirked.

Green-and-white Boston Celtics shorts. A red-and-blue New England Patriots T-shirt. I looked like a walking crayon box.

The hum of the ceiling fan filled the quiet as I tried to piece together the night before. The louder the music got, the more I realized—I wasn't alone.

Soft footsteps approached the doorway. Instinctively, I pulled the blanket up to my neck just as Naomi leaned against the frame.

Pink apron. Cartoonish smiley face. And underneath? My old college football jersey.

The oversized fabric drowned her, hitting just above her knees. Her hair was pulled into a simple ponytail, no makeup, just radiant, natural beauty that somehow made me gasp.

"Good morning, sleepyhead." She grinned, arms crossed, waiting.

I stared, my brain scrambling for answers. Nothing concrete surfaced. Did we sleep in the same bed? Worse—did we... do anything?

My heart pounded as I searched her face for clues, but Naomi was as unreadable as ever. She leaned in, her breath warm against my cheek as she brushed a thumb across my jaw.

"Breakfast will be ready in a few. Get cleaned up, and I'll see you soon, okay?"

Then she was gone, her voice blending effortlessly with the gospel music as she sauntered back to the kitchen. Meanwhile, I sat frozen, my mind racing.

What happened last night?

I needed answers. Fast.

Rolling out of bed, I took a quick shower, brushed my teeth, and threw on fresh clothes. As I stepped into the dining room, my eyes widened at the spread—French toast, crispy bacon, egg whites, a fresh bowl of fruit. A jug of Simply orange juice sat next to a steaming pot of coffee. My stomach growled in approval.

"This looks amazing," I said under my breath, but before I could dig in, a thought hit me—where was my phone?

Retracing my steps, I found it laying across the bed. Grabbing it, I tapped the screen, and a message lit up from **Alexis**.

> Good morning, JB. I hope you slept well. I've been up all night, thinking.

My brows pulled together as I scrolled down.

> Last night, my ex and I had a long talk—one of those talks that changed everything. Through all the hurt and confusion, we found a way back to each other. We've decided to give our relationship another chance. I'm sorry if this feels sudden or
>
> unfair, but I had to be honest. Meeting you? You made me question everything. You're kind, genuine, and something about you feels real. But in the end, my heart is pulling me back to him.

I exhaled sharply, shaking my head. Break up with me? We weren't even dating.

Then my eyes caught the last part.

> P.S. I think Pastor Naomi has feelings for you. And, James? I've noticed how you look at her, too. I'm not mad—actually, I

think you two would make a great couple. Just so you know, she's been divorced for over **ten years.**

I stared at the words, my mind blank. Then, without warning, a laugh surfaced. It started small, then rolled out of me in waves.

"Something funny?" Naomi's voice pulled me back. She was standing by the table, pouring juice, apron slightly crooked from the morning's cooking spree.

I set my phone down. "Yeah. Everything's great."

I went to fill our glasses when something caught my eye—her left hand.

Bare.

No ring.

I froze.

**Wait.**

From the moment we crossed paths in church, I convinced myself she was married—someone else's wife. I built a wall around my feelings, refusing to let them surface, because wanting her felt wrong.

But she *wasn't* married.

She had never been—not in the time I had known her.

The truth hit me like a freight train. Every time she had tried to tell me, I had found a way to miss it.

A phone call. A knock at the door. A shift in conversation.

Or maybe… I had been avoiding it.

Because knowing she was available meant facing something bigger. Something undeniable.

I had always *loved* Naomi. And I had spent all this time lying to myself.

I stood abruptly, my heart racing, as I walked toward her. Naomi barely had time to react before I wrapped my arms around her, holding her close.

"What was that for?" she asked, looking up at me.

I exhaled, my grip tightening. "I *love* you, Naomi."

And then, before I could second-guess it, **I kissed her.**

Really *kissed* her.

It was like breaking a dam, releasing everything I hadn't even realized was there. Her body tensed for a half-second, then melted into mine. Her fingers curled into my shirt, a quiet gasp escaping against my mouth before she kissed me back. Really kissed me back.

The world faded—the food, the morning light, the lingering confusion. *None of it mattered.*

When we finally pulled apart, her cheeks were flushed, and her eyes sparkled with unshed tears. Slowly, she reached into her shirt and pulled out a delicate silver chain with a heart-shaped pendant featuring a tiny lock.

The **key**.

I blinked as she held it up, and without a word, I reached into my own shirt to reveal the silver chain she had given me. At the end of it hung the *key*—the key to unlock her *heart*. Her eyes said *finally* as we stood there, breathing the same air, the pieces of our unspoken story finally aligning.

In that sacred moment, I realized that God doesn't always show us things the way they seem at first. Love isn't just about what we see or feel on the surface—it's a ***hidden exchange***, deeper, more real, and more true than we could ever understand on our own.

For the first time in a long time, I was ready to embrace what I had been running from.

I was *home*.

Read on for an excerpt from **The Hidden Oath**...

**The Hidden Oath**...

Book 2 of The **Hidden** Trilogy

# Excerpt from **The Hidden Oath**

THE CROWD BEGAN TO QUIET, EYES TURNING UP TO meet mine. I cleared my throat and let a small smile play on my face. Here I was, running on fumes, staring down a room full of students with the smell of coffee in the air and a thousand thoughts spinning in my head. But for the first time in days, the anxiety melted away, replaced by a hint of anticipation.

"Good afternoon, everyone! Thank you for having me here today. It's inspiring to be in a room filled with people who represent the future—people with energy, creativity, and big dreams. You're all here because you've worked hard, and now you're standing on the edge of an exciting new chapter.

Thank you also to the dean of this fine university. I'll let you in on a little secret, though—I only met Dean Jacobs this morning. I know he said we were good friends, but…" Everyone laughed. "We're not really friends, but I'm sure he's a *great* guy!"

Just as I was about to start, I spotted the old woman again, waving subtly to get my attention. Her eyes were fixed on me, intense, like she had something to say. For a second, I felt thrown off, but I shook it off, looked past her, and began my speech.

"I graduated at the top of my class from one of the best universities in the country," I began, letting the words settle in. "I was a celebrated athlete. And, well, I wasn't exactly unpopular with the ladies, either." The crowd laughed, loosening up a little. "But I'm not here to talk about my achievements. I'm here to talk about my mistakes—because those are what truly shaped me."

A few faces perked up, curious. I continued, "After college, I started running with some tough people. The kind of guys that, if you passed them on the street, you might think about crossing to the other side. A nine-to-five job just seemed too... *ordinary*, so I got into things I never should have—selling drugs, robbing dealers, stealing cars."

I saw shock ripple across the crowd. Perfect. I had their attention.

"I look back now and wonder why I chose that path when a better one was right in front of me. I think it's because I felt lost. I grew up in a single-parent household, with two older brothers who were tough as nails, ruling the streets in their own way. They taught me how to be strong, how to fight. I wanted to be just like them—but with a college degree." The room fell silent, every eye locked on me.

"It wasn't until eight years ago, when I was 23, that I got the call that shattered my life. My mother told me my oldest brother had been murdered. He was standing outside his own house with friends when a car pulled up, and someone fired six shots into him." I felt a tear slip free, and as I brushed it away, I noticed others in the audience wiping their eyes, too. "I wanted revenge so badly I could taste it. But then, I remembered my brother's last words to me: 'Whatever you do, live your life. Give your best to everything. Don't be like me.'

"In that moment, everything I thought I wanted fell away. His words became my guide. I realized toughness alone wasn't enough—it was the choices I made that would shape my life. His choices led him to that end, and it could have been me. It could be any one of you sitting here today. Your choices today will shape your future, so choose wisely."

I paused, letting it sink in.

"Each of you has the power to build a future better than the one I was heading toward. Some of you will go on to be doctors, lawyers, or therapists. Some might start off working at McDonald's or Wendy's. But remember, it's not where you start—it's the life you choose to create. You decide what kind of future you'll have."

Looking out at the crowd, I saw young faces filled with possibility. "When I see this room, I don't just see students. I see future leaders—people who can change their communities, bring compassion into the world, and inspire others. That's the power of your choices."

Twenty minutes later, I finished, placed the microphone back on its stand, and returned to my seat. The room erupted into a standing ovation that seemed to last forever.

*Mission accomplished.*